Most of my cases were straight-forward, but this one was filled with treachery that could get us all killed...

Ian came forward to sit next to me among several rows of empty seats. "If you don't mind," he said, "I'd like to talk over something with you quietly."

I waited, watching out the window as a fairytale land of vineyards faded into the watercolor distance and half-timbered villages looked freshly-minted from *Snow White* or *Cinderella*. I reminded myself that all of it could be gone in a nuclear flash.

"Has Walt recruited you?" Fleming asked in hushed tones. "Or are you a lone hand? You seem very capable."

I waited some more. He and Walt had seemed so confident, cool, and sure that they were doing the right thing. It was a marvel, given the circumstances.

'*So many people have a hidden side*,' the Noir Man told me.

"How would you like to operate unofficially for the British Secret Service?" Ian asked. "On American soil, of course."

I raised my eyebrows for something to do. "Are you trying to recruit me to spy on my own country?"

"Well, let us call it a liaison. Her Majesty needs information from a variety of sources, particularly in Hollywood."

In October 1959, someone is out for revenge against young Los Angeles PI, Stan Wade, who has solved a few cases for his main client, Walt Disney. When a CIA agent mistakenly dies in Stan's place, Stan initiates a revenge investigation that leads him outside the country, and his own comfort zone, to stop a nuclear threat to Europe that will remain classified until 2012.

KUDOS for *Spyfall*

In *Spyfall* by John Hegenberger, Stan Wade is an LA PI in 1959. His main client is Walt Disney, who he refers to as Uncle Walt. This time, Uncle Walt wants him to act as a liaison between the Mob and the author of the James Bond novels, Ian Fleming. But what seems like a simple case turns out to be much more complicated, involving spies, assassins, and some very dark secrets. Hegenberger has crafted a fun read. It's exciting, clever, and chock full of surprises. I heartily recommend it. ~ *Taylor Jones, Reviewer*

Spyfall by John Hegenberger is an historical mystery-espionage-thriller. Our hero, Stan Wade, is a PI working out of a small office in LA in 1959. But while he may be small time, he has some big clients, most notably Uncle Walt, who is none other than Walt Disney. So Stan, his partner/apprentice Norm, Walt Disney, and author Ian Fleming of James Bond fame travel to Europe and East Germany to save the world. Naturally. According to the author's note at the back of the book, the story is based on things that actually happened. If that is the case, then at that time, Walt Disney was into a lot more than Mickey Mouse! *Spyfall* is extremely well-written for a debut novel. The characters are charming and intriguing, the plot is strong, and the action is fast-paced enough to keep you turning pages. ~ *Regan Murphy, Reviewer*

SPYFALL

John Hegenberger

A Black Opal Books Publication

Black Opal Books

BECAUSE SOME STORIES JUST HAVE TO BE TOLD

GENRE: HISTORICAL SPY THRILLER/MYSTERY-DETECTIVE

SPYFALL
Copyright © 2015 by John Hegenberger
Cover Design by John Hegenberger
All cover art copyright © 2015
All Rights Reserved
Print ISBN: 978-1-626944-21-3

First Publication: OCTOBER 2015

Published by Black Opal Books **http://www.blackopalbooks.com**

DEDICATION

For the real Molly Oddi, my daughter

"Three years before the Cuban missile crisis, the Soviet Union had already placed nuclear weapons on foreign soil, in this wood in what was then East Germany...But it is also now known that the missiles deployed in East Germany in spring 1959 were suddenly withdrawn later in the year, unbeknownst to the CIA..." ~ *BBC News Magazine* October 25, 2012

Let's all remember that what follows is a work of "faction" based entirely on the author's dreams, recollections, and speculations. None of the names have been changed to protect anyone. All of the events *almost* occurred exactly as reported.

PART I
GOLDEN OAK

CHAPTER 1

Sometimes people tell you the damnedest things, hoping you'll believe them.

"You're the dirty rat who killed my brother," Frank Gorshin intoned. "And now I'm going to rub you out, see?"

It was a warm Friday afternoon, September 25, 1959 at 12:45 PM, as I sat in my windowless office at the back of the Brown Derby and listened to the gangly actor/impressionist. It may have been warm outside, but it was positively steaming in this cramped room next to the restaurant's overheated and noisy kitchen.

"Not bad," I said, preparing to make notes in a little book I carried. I'd recently taken to jotting down the facts, ma'am, for fear I'd forget them. "Now do Boris Karloff."

Gorshin leaned forward in the client chair, slumped his shoulders, and lisped, "Protozoa—taking over my lab-or-atory."

I'd had very few clients and a couple of rough months recently. My car needed major repairs and the same was true for the leaky boat moored near the Del Rey swamps, which I called home. Add in my medical expenses from a case I'd worked earlier in the week for Walt during Khrushchev's visit to the set of *Can-Can*, and you'll understand why I'd begun to consider even a night security job at the Dodger Stadium construction site as a golden employment opportunity.

"Can you do Kate Hepburn?" I asked, distracted by the sweat that trickled down my spine and thoughts of lunch. The heavy tang of cooked cabbage and flame-grilled T-bones drifted in from the nearby stoves and ovens.

Gorshin started in about calla lilies blooming, but I cut him off with a, "Wait. What, if anything, has this to do with the bank robbery you mentioned?"

He tilted his head to one side and winced up at me, sounding like Kirk Douglas. "Don't you see?" he wheezed. "I'm being framed. Someone's impersonating me."

Who ever heard of a celebrity imitator being imper-sonated? Frankly, I thought it was ridiculous. My friends were beginning to say that I felt that way about a lot of things.

They'd taken to calling me a smartass. I guess they were half right, but I wasn't sure which half.

"Look, Mr. Gorshin," I said, trying to appear more impressed than I felt. "I'll assign one of our best operatives to follow-up with you on this case for our usual fee." I looked at the watch my brother had given me before his death at the Battle of Midway. I'd worn it for years, partly as tribute to Josh and partly to tell the time. "I'm sure we can help you, but at the moment I'm late for a meeting with the FBI. You understand, of course."

I was trying to sound important. Unfortunately, the head of the restaurant, Robert Cobb, chose that moment to stick his head in and say that he wanted to see me now that I'd shown up for work. The Derby let me keep an office here, such as it was, rent free here in exchange for my services as a quasi-bouncer and tab-collector.

My prospective client was staring at the jumble of napkin dispensers on top of my lone file cabinet. He tightened his right eye, fixing me with it. "You sure you're a private dick? What's this going to cost me?"

My darker side whispered, "A million dollars."

"Not too much." I smiled. "Usually fifty bucks a day with the first three days in advance. Okay?"

He got out his wallet with a "Hmmm" and paid me in cash. "When can your operative start?"

My noir side silently said, '*When he comes back from the movies.*'

I figured Norman to be just about finished taking in

the double horror matinee at the Pantages about now. Something involving a fly and an alligator man. My pal, Norm would have sold his back teeth and possibly his brain for a chance to meet Vincent Price.

"Please write down your address, Mr. Gorshin," I said, holding my smile and handing him my notebook and an unchewed pencil. "Oh, and your phone number, too. Our Mr. Norman Weirick will contact you. Probably in the morning."

A few minutes later, we parted company, not the best of friends, and I pocketed his cash before ducking Cobb and grabbing half a ham sandwich on my way through the kitchen's rear exit.

The melodic tones of a nearby jack hammer blended with those of an insistent car horn on Wilshire to fill the warm, smoggy air of the parking lot. I added to the urban symphony by sneezing twice and gunning the engine of my rusty Kaiser. A couple of Spanish kids roller-skated past, giving me the bird.

This is the city. My name is Stan Wade. I'm not a cop. I'm not even a private investigator. The LAPD pulled my license months ago. Dumb-da-dumb-damn.

ᕙᕗᕙᕗ

I headed west for the *Cervantes II*, while listening to the Dodgers play the Cubs on the car radio. I knew, of course, who Cervantes was—author of *Don Quixote*—but

I figured that the boat's original owner had named her after something more prosaic, like the road near the marina up in San Francisco where the ship had been constructed.

Like a lot of Angelinos, I'd become a fan of our new baseball team, and it looked like we had a decent shot at the Series if Larry Sherry's pitching arm held out. As I steered onto Santa Monica Boulevard and hit a petrified forest of traffic, I switched the radio off and reached under the dashboard for the car-phone Norman had installed there. It wasn't really a phone—more like a fancy walky-talky—but I could call Norm and he could transfer me to other people by connecting with the actual phone at his end. Norm's a smart guy, but a little weird. He'd recently quit his job at A1 Electronics, because he was certain that his boss was a "commie."

Now he wanted to be a private eye, while writing murder mysteries from his apartment on Boylston, over near Elysian Park.

When his voice finally struggled through the static-filled connection, he started right in with the lyric game. "You reach the Pennsylvania station 'bout a quarter to four. Read a magazine and then you're in Baltimore."

The game was for each of us to challenge other with popular songs from the past, usually show tunes. I immediately answered with, "Dinner in the diner. Nothing could be finer than to have your ham and eggs in Carolina."

He chuckled. "That one was too easy. What's up, boss?"

"How was the movie?"

"Shocking. They switched the bill, so I got to see *The Tingler* instead and my seat was wired with Percepto."

I had no idea what he was talking about. Sometimes Norm was as goofy as Garry Moore. He looked a bit like him too, when he wasn't wearing his thick specks. I gave him the details about the Gorshin case and he immediately promised to look into it.

As I neared the gravel parking lot near the slip where my boat was moored, he told me he had a title for his new crime novel, *My Gun is Sneaky*, and asked me to read the opening chapters. This was another game we played. He wrote and I read, offering insight and opinions in lieu of a salary, while he learned the basics of detection.

"Okay. I'll come by tomorrow and pick up the manuscript while you report what you've learned about Gorshin."

"'Nothing could be finer,'" he quoted. "Over and out."

The phone spat an electric buzz at me. I signed off and waved a hand to Max Beeler, waiting for me at the pier.

"Hey, Streak," he said, shaking my hand and gazing at the top of my head. "Why don't you dye that thing, before people start thinking you're a skunk?"

I didn't let him see me wince from either the comment or the handshake, but I couldn't stop myself from touching the patch of white that flowed back from my scalp. "And I didn't think you people used Brylcreem, but your hair has that shine." I gave his shoulder a short punch. "Good to see you again, Max. Come on aboard."

Max was my height, thickset, but generally better looking than me, even though his skin had the texture and color of a wet potato. He wore a light brown suit and black knit tie with an overhand knot. I'd met him months earlier during an undercover operation in Vegas.

We sat in the shade of the wheel-house, drinking glasses of iced Pepsi from my galley and listening to a Top 40 station on the radio that quietly played "Mac the Knife." A single seabird floated on the breeze, then swooped down to snatch up something from the water's surface and sail away.

Max sweetened his pop with the contents of a silver flask from his coat pocket. Our ice cubes tinkled when we toasted to crime and the flask clanked against the butt of his gun when he put it back under his shoulder.

I looked down at a small hole in my tie where I'd accidently burned it months earlier. A lot of my shirts and a couple of my pants legs had similar pinholes from fallen ashes. Well, not any more. I'd stopped smoking earlier in the year and my sinuses would forever thank me. At the same time, I'd saved a couple of bucks each week, too. "Life is good," I told Max, "when you live it right."

He nodded and ran a palm along nearby port railing. "Wish I could live like this all the time. Fresh sea air and the gentle rocking of the waves." He sighed. "My she's yar."

I was impressed that he knew the term. "Aye, that she is. But you didn't come here to admire sleek watercraft. What's on your mind?"

He took a long pull on his drink. "Walt found a bomb in his car yesterday. So did I. We think Reed's brother, Nicolas, planted them."

"Revenge?"

"Exactly." Max's favorite phrase.

"I didn't know Reed had a brother."

August Reed had tried to crater a major part of Southern California a few months ago. I had been part of an undercover FBI operation that had stopped him— dead.

"The Bureau has a very thin dossier on Brother Nicolas, except that he's currently believed to be here in LA." He pointed his chin back toward shore. "We should probably check that rust bucket of yours. Just to be safe."

I said, "Exactly," and we got up and walked back to the parking lot. Except for Max's Ford, which he'd parked beside a tilting phone pole and couple of skiffs overturned and baking in the sun, my Kaiser sat alone, waiting near the gangway of the *Cervantes II*. It seemed more threatening than before, like a dozing bull.

I let Max pop the hood and we both peeked inside.

There was a small tan box, wires, and a soft-ball-sized lump of grey clay strapped behind the left headlight. Definitely non-standard equipment.

"That's a timer," Max said, pointing at the tan box. "Just like the one that was in my car. Could have been placed there any time in the last twenty-four hours. Better stand away while I disconnect it."

I took a couple of steps back. "You sure you know what you're—"

"Got it," he called out, still bent over the engine. "Whew."

"Whew is right," he said, still working at the device. "I'm sweating like a pig out here in the sun."

"I don't think it's the sun that's making you sweat."

"Exactly."

Max and the front end of my Kaiser flew up in a roaring, rolling ball of yellow flame that threw me back and down on my left side. Gravel bit into my skin and a piece of the car's hood slammed down silently next to my face and bounced away.

CHAPTER 2

I coughed until I almost lost it. Shaken and deafened by the concussion, I staggered to my hands and knees and saw the top half of Max Beeler blown to bloody shreds across the parking lot.

A crowd started to gather, drawn by the explosion. One guy in a red-and-white horizontal striped pullover, clamped onto me as if to help me stay erect, but I think he was shouting to everyone that I was to blame. My ears rang and I could only faintly hear the sirens wail as a fire-truck and ambulance arrived.

A patrolman took me away from the Beagle Boy and we went over to lean on the side of Max's Galaxie. The Ford's hot surface burned my arm and I noticed that one of the side windows had a thin sliver from my Kaiser's grill stuck in the glass, as if it had been propelled there by a knife thrower. Somewhere along the way, I'd acquired a silver flask. I paused a moment to slowly touch it to my forehead in a silent salute to its owner.

The leaning telephone pole let loose in a delayed reaction, chopping the ground like an axe.

After that, the whole place became a sideshow. Ambulances flashed their colorful lights. Water arced through the air. Crowds of spectators ringed the area. A tent became erected near the remains. A helicopter made a vibrating pass over our heads. Even a van from KTLA-5 showed up to film the still-smoking wreckage.

I was hustled along to my boat, but before the cops could start questioning me, a thin wiry guy in a dark suit—who I took to be from the FBI—flashed his wallet and ushered me off to a waiting limo. He mouthed some words, including ones that looked like "white dizzy," and the driver sped me away from the crazy circus.

Twenty minutes later, I had most of my hearing back, but was still a little dazed. My hand shook as I plucked a scrap of moist brown cloth from the sleeve of my coat.

The dark limo dropped me off inside a familiar complex of studios in Burbank. I walked down Mickey Avenue past the commissary to the administration offices. The smell of freshly-clipped grass brought me down out of an adrenaline haze. Buddy Ebsen shuffled past me, humming to himself and going the other way. I remembered how Fess Parker had once threatened to have me arrested for loitering while I was on stakeout near his home. My Noir Man said, '*What a crockett shit.*'

Inside the ochre, stucco three-story, I asked to see Walt. I was beginning to get my wits back and, like a trained observer, began noticing details around me. Beth, a pudgy brunette in a French Twist and a little too much eye makeup, rose from the reception desk and straightened the front of her skirt, smiling. She recognized me from previous visits, seemed to have expected me today, and directed me to the Animation Building over on Buena Vista Street.

I found the building, went up the stairs, and spied Walt standing at the back of a large, high-windowed room, addressing more than a dozen artists seated at their work tables. One guy was sketching Peter Pan for a peanut butter commercial. Another sat in the bright sunlight and drew a bucktoothed beaver holding a toothbrush. Maybe I was still a little dopey, after all.

Walt was wearing his reading glasses and calmly assuring a hunched-shouldered man of about fifty that even though live-action movies were now the bulk of the company's production, he would never abandon animation. "It's in my heart and soul, Leo." The studio head spread wide his arms, one of which almost poked a cigarette into the eye of a lean guy in a polo shirt.

Which was another good reason why I'd stopped smoking.

Walt caught sight of me standing at the room's entrance and came past me into the hallway. "This way."

I followed his back as he stubbed out his cigarette and opened a door at the end of the hall.

We went into an empty workroom—empty except for walls filled with images from *Sleeping Beauty* and three wooden desks covered with stacks of similar drawings. No chairs, so I just stood there while he closed the door and went over to look out the window before closing the horizontal blinds.

"Stan," he said, taking off his glasses and slipping them into interior pocket of his tweed sport coat.

"Walt."

"Are you all right?"

"Are you?"

He blinked. "What do you mean?"

"Max is dead." I took the flask from my pocket and set it on the nearest desk. I wobbled a little but stayed upright.

"I know," Walt said, his eyes glued to the silver surface. "I sent the limo that brought you here, remember. The police will want a statement, but we'll pull rank on them and cover you for the time being. We've got a line on who did this and why.

"I was almost killed by my car!"

"And we're going to get the man who did it. I know you're upset—"

"My parents died in their car ten years ago, remember?"

"And we found a bomb in my car, too."

"Whose fault is that, Mr. Secret Agent?"

Walt waited while the echo of my voice faded. "You seem tired, Stan. Maybe—maybe it would be best, if you went out of town for a while. While the Bureau clears this up."

"You're not listening, Walt. There are people out there who are trying to kill us."

"They term they use is eliminate or liquidate."

"Whatever it is, I'm not running away."

He ran his fingers through his hair. "Look, I'm sick about what happened to Max. But I'm glad that you're safe. We didn't know that Reed had a brother. Our records are sketchy at best, but I received a call two days ago saying we were all going to pay for August Reed's death and something about 'blood calls to blood.'"

"And?"

"And, we tried to trace the call, but weren't expecting it to begin with and fully—got nowhere."

I wondered how the caller knew about Max's and my involvement in the death of August Reed. "Someone inside the FBI is leaking information."

"Probably," Walt said. "Possibly. We're looking into it. The fact that he called to warn me first tells us that he's bold and clearly out for revenge. The profiles from Bureau psychologists state that a call like that is designed to instill fear, even at the risk of exposure. When the threat is carried out on any one member of a group, the rest of the members begin to panic."

"Well, it only motivates me to want to get them before they get me like they did Max."

"And that sort of reaction is precisely what the psych boys describe as panic. You want to drop everything and run off in all directions at once. We can't do that, Stan. We have active, on-going cases that have to be pursued methodically. We have to keep our wits. We can't be stampeded like spooked cattle."

"Are you going to quote Davy Crockett to me, now? 'Be sure you're right and then go ahead'? How do we do that methodically, Walt?"

"By keeping our heads, and keeping them down. You know we have resources to handle this sort of thing. I dealt with something very much like this back in the Forties."

"Max Beeler was a good man. And you're not telling me everything—again."

He sighed. "He'll be missed. I'd like to have a lengthy conversation with you about it, but right now…" I could see the complexity of conflicting thoughts play across his face. "As you say, there's a lot I haven't told you."

I waited while he weighed how much to explain. "I want to hear it all," I said. "You owe me that."

He slumped. "This damn business gets harder every year. Your parents had high-level security clearances while working on projects at Lockheed after the war. They were presented to me one day in 1947 as part of a team to keep the atomic bomb out of soviet hands."

I clinched my eyes, hoping they didn't water, and the Noir Man screamed at the back of my throat.

CHAPTER 3

Outside the window in the street below, a bus braked to a stop, hissed its doors, and then revved past on its determined route.

Walt took a moment to light a cigarette and then rested himself on the edge of a desk. "At first, the Bureau only wanted me to advise them of any socialist or communist activities that I found in the unions here in Hollywood. Then a high-level official named Donovan asked me to report on other things—sometimes specific individuals and studios and with operations overseas."

I stared him down. "Get to the part where my dad and mom worked for you undercover."

"They worked *with* me, let's say." He plucked a bit of tobacco from his lip. "Your mother was very adept at figuring things out and keeping secrets. I mean that in a good way, of course. Your father was very patriotic. He always had high principles. Wanted to become a priest or something, if I recall correctly. I could be wrong about that, but he was the one who made me swear to look after you, if anything ever happened to them—off the books, you understand."

"No, Uncle Walt," I said with a taste of sarcasm. "That's the problem." No need for the Noir Man here. Things were dark enough. "Explain it to me."

He appeared to be counting to ten before going on. "Look, Stan. You'll have to extrapolate some of my meaning. Even now, I can't—"

"Dammit, did you send them out to be killed? Did you cause their deaths?"

"No. God, no." He wanted me to believe him. "If anything, it was the other way around. You see, the Lockheed plant has a hidden manufacturing area we called the Skunkworks, where advance-designed aircraft were developed and tested for defense. That's how I first got involved with the OSS—through your parents and what they were doing there to foil our enemies."

I kept my voice level. "Foil our enemies. You mean the Communists?"

"Yes—for the most part. Your parents were loyal Americans, Stan, but their work had to be kept secret, even from you. When they, uh, passed away, you were starting college. I did all I could to help you through your loss. I wanted to do more, but my hands were tied by the

Bureau. We couldn't risk exposing you to the dangers that had taken your parents."

"The less I knew, the safer I'd be. Is that it?" He gave me a half-smile and started to speak, but I cut him off with, "That's obscene, Walt. You kept me in the dark and fed me horse shit, like one of your cartoon toadstools."

"No. I gave you a dream. A second chance. You wanted to be an investigator, so I set it up that you could learn from one of the best. 'A dream is a wish your heart makes—'"

"Stop with the silly symphony lyrics." I raised my voice. "You're telling me that Mr. P took me on because you asked him to?"

"Actually, no. He didn't like the idea at all and hesitated at first, but you were eager and showed strong promise. That determination and dedication has allowed me to employ you un-officially on assignments over the last few years, which is why I want you to have this." He reached into his coat pocket and held out a thin wallet.

I stared at the FBI credentials that displayed my name.

His voice softened. "I know you lost your PI license, so perhaps this will—"

"You had this faked up by someone in one of your art departments, didn't you?"

"Lord, you're suspicious."

"Do you blame me?"

He waited for me to calm down and then further extended the black leather thing. "I had a devil of a time getting that approved. You'll still need to go through some formal training before it's official, but you've earned it, Stan. A reward for services rendered thus far."

The lines of his face deepened above his broad square jaw. His eyebrows wrinkled his forehead. Mustache neatly trimmed. Hair combed straight back. Breast-pocket handkerchief sharp enough to cut cheese. The picture of American free enterprise.

I tossed the wallet onto the desktop where it went *flup*. "And what if I no longer what to be played?"

I think I heard his teeth grit. "Then I've done all I can for you."

The statement hung in the air. He had done a lot for me, but it had always been from the shadows and for our mutual benefit. I got a case and he got results. By rights, I should be mildly grateful, but I still couldn't bring myself to completely trust him. I felt like a hired gun—which was part of the business I was in and we both knew it.

I pushed the Noir Man down and said, "I'll need some time to think it over."

His expression didn't brighten. He was all business and matter-of-fact when he answered. "Granted. And in the meantime, I'd like to hire you as before at double rates to check in with an acquaintance of mine who's in town and needs your expertise."

"My expertise," I said, "for what?"

He brought something else from his pocket and handed it over—a slip of paper with *While You Were Out* printed at the top. "He's staying at the Biltmore for a day or so in the room written there, registered as a Mr. Birds from England. Birds is not his real name."

"What's his problem?"

"He's an interesting novelist, but his books have relied on organized crime as the villains. The Mafia doesn't like that, I hear, and they want him to stop. They've become very image-conscious lately. I know you have a few solid connections with the local mob, so you can possibly advise him how to deal with the problem."

It all sounded lame to me. Walt could be like that. As if he was giving me something to distract me from more critical issues.

"Like I said," I told him, moving to the door, "I'll think about it. I'm going down to the street. Call your chauffer and get me out of this puzzle palace." It felt good to leave him standing there surrounded by images from his own fantasies.

Back out on Buena Vista, I waited for the limo. The sun warmed the back of my neck and a slight breeze cooled my temper. It was another beautiful California day, but I still felt ugly and manipulated.

I looked down at the note Walt had given me. The name written there rang a distant bell, but I had more important things on my mind than the woes of some British writer called Ian Fleming.

cɔɛɔ

I directed the limousine driver to drop me off up in the hills near the Hollywood Bowl. Suzi's apartment was my home away from home and I'd been spending more time here lately than on my boat.

Still ruminating over what Walt had said, I noticed two small birds were roosting on the roof antenna of her simple two-story brick building. There was dark blue wooden trim at every entranceway. Her mailbox displayed the word "Sunset" in white letters impacted into a strip of red label tape. I had a key, but rang the bell to show that I cared.

"Here, take this," she said, after I'd been with her for a few minutes.

"What is it?"

"Four-Way Cold tablet." Her earrings were tiny blue disks that matched her eyes.

"I don't have a cold. I have a four-way allergy to your dumb cat."

"Phooey's not dumb. He's lovable. Now swallow that and you'll feel better."

To me, Suzi was a combination of the best parts of Julie London, Lola Albright, and Tuesday Weld. Obviously, I was mixed up about her.

I got the pill down with a swig of tap water, but it still tasted bitter. I sneezed to prove her wrong about the cure and stared hard at the golden fur-ball who sat curled in a living room chair, clogging my sinuses. "He's a public menace. I'm the one who's lovable."

She leaned over and kissed the top of my head. "Yes, you are, Standy." Her eyes crinkled when she lingered on my pet name. "When you're asleep."

I let her get away with the gag and only said, "Hey!"

"I know you're upset about what Walt told you."

"Or didn't tell me."

"But you've got to work through it. It's not all that bad."

I took a breath. I hadn't told her about the explosion and Max's death. It felt better to keep her out of it for now. Maybe tomorrow.

She had changed her hair again. It was still blonde and neatly trimmed, but now there were delicate bangs caressing her forehead. Seemed like a good idea to me.

"So," I said, still waiting for the pill to kick in, "how was your day?"

She gave me her patented killer smile and plunked down playfully next to me on the lounge in front of the TV. She had the most modernly-furnished apartment I'd ever seen and a pair of eyes sometimes innocent and sometimes bottomless.

"I'm working on an inquiry for Bill Crump."

"Who?"

"You probably know him as Blake Edwards."

"The guy who writes *Peter Gunn* and *Richard Diamond*?"

"And a bunch of other things like, *Mr. Lucky*."

"Oh, yeah. I like that Andamo character. What's the case about?"

She smiled with pools of sleepy blue. "Someone's holding his dog for ransom."

"Yikes. A dog-napping case. Alert the media."

"Hey, they can't all be high-profile gang-busters, you know. At least, it keeps the lights burning at the agency."

Suzi had once been my competitor in the investigation racket, but lately we'd worked together and played together so often that we were almost partners. In fact, she had taken me on as an op at her agency after, and even though, the cops had pulled my PI ticket. Even more to the fact, we planned to get married soon, which was why her place felt like home to me.

"So, who done it?" I asked. "And what are you going to do about it."

She punched a button on the remote and the TV started to hum. "I'm not sure yet. There seems to be a young actor involved named Clu Gulager."

I said, "A name you can clean your teeth with."

She ignored me as we caught the commercials at the end of the *Perry Como Show*. "I think he's related to Will Rogers."

"Hmmm…" I said, watching a fascinating ad for cheese-spread. My mind kept going back to what Walt had told me about my parents.

I repeated the key points again to Suzi, who listened

quietly and then handed me her new Princess phone.

"What's this?"

"Call him."

"Who? Mr. P? It's early afternoon in Hawaii. He'll be out, or napping, or out in the Hawaiian sun—napping."

"Call him anyway. It's the only way you'll know if Walt was telling the truth."

I still hesitated. What bothered me was that I just might learn that Mr. P had been hiding the truth from the start. If so, I'd feel even more betrayed.

Suzi took the phone back and said, "What's his number?"

Somebody, perhaps the Noir Man, got out my notebook and showed her the long distance information scribbled there.

She dialed and we waited, watching the TV. A woman on *What's My Line* stumped the panel with her job selling tickets to the World's Series.

"You're not mad at them," she told me, while the circuits hummed. "You're mad at yourself for not having pieced it all together from the start."

"Some detective, I am," I said as the phone stopped ringing in my ear and the old man picked up with an "Aloha."

"Hey, boss. It's me."

Mr. P had taken me under his wing almost a decade ago and now I told him that I finally knew why. At the time, I was a dumb kid who idolized detective work. I'd read Chandler and Hammett and a bunch of others and thought that being a private eye was the next thing to heaven. When my folks became senseless victims of a car crash in the Hollywood Hills, I'd desperately sought a way to escape circumstances and rushed to the one dream I'd had that made the world seem right.

My family had known Mr. P for several years, so it wasn't surprising that I'd gravitated toward him after the funeral. I'd told him how I felt about detective work and he seemed to understand. Soon, he had me sifting through files and digging out information that helped him solve a couple of cases. It wasn't glamorous work, but I took to it like a fish takes to smelly bait. I was hooked.

Now, live, from his retirement home in Honolulu, the old man admitted the truth. He confirmed Walt's story of taking me on at Disney's request. "I didn't know all the details about your situation, but I could see that it was the right thing to do, Stan. You were a whiz. And frankly, it came at a time when I wasn't doing so well. I needed an operation on my back and you helped pick up the load while I was down."

Suzi sat near, watched my expression, and tried to listen in. I tilted the edge of the phone receiver so she could hear the tiny, metallic voice from the islands.

Mr. P apologized for not telling me sooner. "Honestly, it wasn't a problem, Stan. Not to me anyway. You were your own man and a hell of an investigator. You stood your ground and waded through the muck to find the answers and help people. That's why I turned the agency over to you when I retired. You earned it, Stan."

It went on like that for another couple of minutes. Him talking. Me listening. Suzi watching. It was all good to hear, but I still felt conflicted and told him the same thing I'd told Walt. "I'll think about it."

His voice broke up from the bad connection, so we rang off.

I just sat there, silently arguing with myself.

Suzi continued to wait.

Finally, I said, "Why would they keep this from me for so long?"

She placed a hand on my knee. "There's no answer for that, Standy. And it's only when you stop asking that it gets quiet inside."

Then she changed the subject by suggesting dinner at my favorite restaurant, the Villa Capri, adding, "And I have passes to a preview at MGM."

I went along with it, for now. Still, it didn't add up. But I decided not to let it ruin our evening.

Dinner was great, as usual, and so was the company. I saw Roger Moore at the bar with a trim brunette on his arm and tried to recall the name of his character on *The Alaskans*. Slinky or Slimy? Just another Brit, like that Fleming guy.

But the Noir Man kept pitching questions at me. Had Walt been successful in tracking down and stopping

Reed's brother? When and where would Max's funeral be? What was I going to do for a car now?

Suzi continued to lighten my mood as she drove us over to MGM Studios on Washington Boulevard. At the gate, she flashed her preview pass to the guard and parked beside several other cars next to a tiny theatre at the back of the lot. We walked to the theater's entrance where an attendant checked her name on a clipboard and gave us each a five-by-seven card to capture our comments.

I'd been to one of these previews before. The studio gave out passes to test a movie in production by asking the sample audience for their opinions before the film's full release. Sometimes, if the comments came back so negative, major changes were made to the movie. Sometimes not.

I didn't know what film we were to see, until the curtain parted, and I recognized the lush, heady overture that had to be the work of Miklos Rozsa. Within minutes, we were in ancient Egypt with *Ben Hur*. Within hours, we were done and out.

Near the end of the picture, the audience had collectively gasped as a charioteer was thrown and trampled beneath a team of thundering horses. I was pretty sure I saw the director, Willy Wyler, slouched down in the row of seats in front of us, keenly watching the crowd's reaction to the death scene.

He seemed to smile.

During the drive back to her apartment, Suzi and I discussed the gruesome scene.

"It looked like a real death to me," she said.

"Imagine if word like that got out," I mused, captured by her stunning profile. "It could kill the movie."

"It could ruin MGM," she said, executing a perfect parallel parking maneuver on the street in front of her building. "I hear that the studio is almost bankrupt again."

"Worse than that," I said. "It could damage the image of the US, if the world thought we were pandering a real death scene to an international audience."

She shivered. I reached a palm over and lightly patted her cheek.

She held my hand next to her face. After a moment, we went inside for a night together. And to hell with the dumb cat, four ways.

CHAPTER 4

We enjoyed and indulged ourselves by sleeping in until 8:30. We shared scrambled eggs and coffee after first sharing a shower. Suzi had to go into the office to work on the Edwards doggy case and she planned to first drop me off at my boat.

Plans changed when we found a suspicious envelope in her mailbox. It had no stamp or return address, but it rattled when shaken. I had her go get a pair of scissors which I used to gingerly cut off a small corner from the envelope. Peering inside, I made out the smiling face of Mickey Mouse chained to a set of car keys.

We walked out to the street and found a new Ford Thunderbird convertible parked directly behind her Renault. It was robin's egg blue and had enough chrome for a thousand toasters.

"Uncle Walt did this," she breathed with awe.

I kicked a whitewall tire next to its spoked hubcap, but didn't answer.

Suzi rattled my hand that held the keys.

I told her to stand back while I looked under the car, into the empty trunk big enough to hold a rowboat, beneath the seats, and under the hood.

She watched and finally asked, "Look safe?"

I pulled at my chin and made a side-to-side "guess-so" gesture with my head.

The engine was a 352-cubic-inch V8 with factory air. The bucket seats were matching pale blue. The interior was tooled leather. The ragtop was white canvas.

The odometer had sixty-four miles on it and the glove-box had the title in it, made out in my name.

"Guess I won't need to be dropped off after all," I said, with a faint grin.

The luscious blonde gave me a hug and a wave and drove off in her mundane vehicle.

I held my breath and started the Bird's engine. It turned over and purred like a toothless Leo the Lion. Since the hood opened backward, I could see the motor from the driver's seat. Everything seemed fine. I closed up the hood and then listened to the servo-motors lower the cloth roof. I put the shiny car into gear and eased out from the curb.

Minutes later, I was doing a smooth fifty in the sun on 101, headed southwest, fiddling with the knobs on the radio to find the Dodgers game. It was the bottom of the fifth and we were behind the Cubs twelve to two. The Noir Man was not happy, but he was never happy about anything.

I got off the freeway at Hope and cut over to Seventh, parking directly in front of the eleven-story Biltmore Hotel's main entrance on Olive Street. As I tossed the keys to an attendant and stopped to take in the lush green on Pershing Square across the street, something there tickled my sinuses and I sneezed.

The doorman tipped his cap and blessed me. Then he whistled lowly and slowly as the big, square T-bird glided away. One damn impressive car, but it drew way too much attention for use by a lowly PI, especially on stakeouts. I'd probably have to sell it or maybe trade it for Suzi's less-noticeable buggy. But not for a while yet. I think I may have been in love.

Once through the revolving glass doors and into the air-conditioned atmosphere of the hotel, my sinuses settled down. The beaux arts interior surrounded and enfolded me, sweeping me up in a mélange of ornate fixtures, intricately-patterned rugs, and murals that would have shamed the Vatican. They once hosted the Academy Awards here and the vast ballroom was known as "Oscar's Home."

Even though there were dozens of people around me, coming and going, the lobby's cavernous expanse high above hung heavily as the hush of a cathedral. There were many sites in LA, especially in Hollywood, that whisked you to another place and time. It's what we do here and our visitors expect it. The Biltmore was one of the most enchanting of these places. Not that it doesn't have a few skeletons in the closets of its roomy suites.

Mr. P once told me that this was the last place the Black Dahlia was seen before her untimely death. That was before my time, but it still sent a chill when I thought of the photos of her severed, nude body. The city and the hotel would probably never live that one down, regardless of all our fancy trappings.

Since I already knew Fleming's room number, I skipped the front desk and went straight for the bank of ornate elevators. I was surprised to see George Reeves in his Clark Kent disguise step out of a descending car, and then quickly recognized as he passed me that it was only Steve Allen.

I got off at Fleming's floor and walked down the oriental carpet. The hallway was crypt-quiet, until I knocked on the gilt-edged door of room 1070. When the door opened and I introduced myself, Fleming reacted the way a lot of people do upon seeing me up close for the first time. He couldn't keep from glancing at the streak of white that ran across my crown. I had a little fun with him by pointing at my face and saying, "My eyes are down here." I could have been less confrontational, but I honestly wasn't in the mood.

"Brown," he said. "What do you want?"

I could see that he wasn't amused and planned to stand his ground at the door. "A mutual friend told me that you were being threatened by a mob—of unfriendly people. I'm here to see if I can help you with that."

"Oh," he said, stepping back. "In that case, do come in. I believe you said your name was Wade."

"That's right." I followed him into a room that carried forward the décor from the lobby, scaled down to less godly proportions.

Fleming stood in the middle of the room, wearing slacks, a smoking jacket, and a bow tie. Any more British and he'd have had a bowler and umbrella. His dull eyes scanned my face. He gestured to one of two dun, high-backed wing chairs that sat beside a cart of premium liquors and fixings. There was a copy of *Playboy* on the floor next to the other chair.

I knew he was a writer and remembered at last where I'd heard of him. Chandler had liked his work, so I decided just then to give one of his books a try when I had the time. But at the moment, I sat and said, "I have a funny feeling that you are our mutual friend's opposite number."

He smiled, sadly. "I'm sure I don't know what you mean by that."

I said, "Yes, of course," and smiled back.

He offered me a drink and I declined with thanks.

It occurred to me that this guy, with his hair thinning and graying at the temples, looked a lot like Walt, only without the moustache. "My understanding is that you're being pressured by the mob to change the way you write. They don't like negative publicity in *any* media."

"That's true," he said, beginning to mix Beefeaters with Roses lime juice.

Even though I'd stopped drinking a few months back, I recognized a gimlet when I saw one being prepared. "They recently stopped production on a Hope and Crosby movie, because the bad guys in the script were supposed to be members of the Syndicate."

He added a wedge of lime to the concoction in his martini glass. "Organized crime still wields incredible power in your country. If they wanted, they could be king makers or president makers. Cheers."

"I assume you don't mean Hope and Crosby."

"No," he said, sipping his drink. "The other chaps— the ones threatening me."

"So why don't you just write them out of your story?"

He set his drink down and almost magically produced a gold cigarette case from the pocket of his smoking jacket. Panache. "How do you mean?"

I leaned forward. "Well, instead of the Mafia, can't you just make the villains some international crime organization?"

"You mean like Fu Manchu?" he asked, lighting what looked like a custom-made cigarette.

"More like, say, the Non-American Terrorist Organization, or something."

"That would have an acronym of NATO."

I looked closely and saw the barest trace of a smile at the corner of the novelist's mouth. "Well, you get the idea," I said.

"Yes," he puffed. "And it's a good one. Something mysterious and worldwide."

"I have connections with a certain Mr. Cohen and can help you get the word out that you're switching bad guys. It might keep the animals off your back."

He sipped his drink again and thought about it. "So if I change the villains into some super-secret cabal, you can tell the local Mob boys and they'll stop the threats."

"Very likely. I've seen it work before." My throat was becoming dry from the smoke and I was beginning to regret not accepting a drink. "They don't want to be featured in the spot light or the lime light."

He politely sniggered at that. "Sort of like rats and roaches," he replied. "I must say, it makes about as much sense as a juggler on the radio, but if it'll work, I'll do it, starting today."

Now, I had to snicker. This guy was quick and clever. "Fine," I said, getting to my feet. "I'll get the word out for you. How long do you expect to remain in our fair city?"

He followed me to the door. "Actually, I'm not supposed to be here at all, you understand. I registered under a false name, because there's a woman in town who desperately wants to see me."

"Yes, of course, there is." I gave him a raised eyebrow. "You can rely on my discretion."

He thanked me and went back to mixing another drink. Mr. Fleming seemed to enjoy many vices.

こうこう

I called Mickey and then Norman from a highly-polished phone booth in the lobby. Norman wanted to sing lyrics at me, but I told him I was busy before ringing off and strolling back out into the September heat. After I retrieved my car from the attendant, the radio reported that the Dodgers had lost and Khrushchev would soon leave New York. I caught a cheeseburger and chocolate malt at Carl's Jr. and dined, driving in luxury. The power steering and power brakes were "ripping."

I now had what I needed from Fleming in order to safely go see Mickey Rat. I'd dealt with him before and was on as good of terms with him as humanly possible, I hoped. He could laugh and still kick you in the balls. For a couple of years now, he'd quietly managed the local bookmakers and enforcers, so that even Joe Friday—let alone Robert Kennedy—couldn't pin anything on the donkey named Cohen.

I recalled that he'd complained to me about Fleming a few months back, calling him a "limey bastard." The

Syndicate wanted to keep their heads down and appear as "respectable businessmen," and if Fleming hadn't lived over in England, they probably would have had a hit out on him. Still...

I drove up San Vicente Boulevard in Brentwood to the swank haberdashery where Mickey once had held court. The quaint men's clothing shop was one of the last places you'd expect him to use as a hang out these days—which was probably why he was there. If the cops found him on premises, they wouldn't pass Go. They'd take him directly to jail, assuming that the cops weren't already collecting $200 from Mickey's payroll.

As I parked, fed the meter, and walked into the shop's entrance, I could feel eyes on me from somewhere. The question was, where they the eyes of hired hoods, hidden police, or someone else. Maybe they were Norman's Tingler using Percepto.

The only patron in the air-conditioned men's store was a guy who looked like Richard Arlen, fingering silk ties on a spinner rack. I'd once been told that I looked like a young Richard Arlen, except for the streak in my hair.

A beefy guy with jowls as dark as Dick Nixon's stood behind a glass counter loaded with tie clasps and cuff links. He glanced up and gave me a hitchhike gesture toward the back room.

Another gent with crocodile-bitten features, who I was pretty sure I'd seen before in mug books, gave me a frisk and then stepped to one side with an open palm.

"Wade-o," Cohen said, not getting up from the hand of rummy he was playing against two overweight thugs in dynamite suits. After all, this was a haberdashery. "Tell me you got good news."

He shifted a cigar from one side of his flat face to the other and waved me nearer. The card players watched my every move like cats. Otherwise, they seemed dead. I hoped they stayed that way.

Despite his expensive outfit and pinky ring, the Mick was starting to show his age. He must have been past fifty by now, but still a showman. There were long lines at his box-office face, deep furrows across the stage of his slick brow, and touches of gray huddled in the longue seats above either ear. Still, he hogged the limelight, regardless of what Fleming had said, performing like a trouper, if not a veteran, partly for me and partly for his gang.

"You're right, Mickey," I said. "I've come with news that Ian Fleming plans to write you guys out of his next book. No more Mafia references in his novels. You guys have been written out."

"Fleming?" he mused, as casual as Como. "Fleming?" "Oh, yeah," he finally announced. "The limey with the spy novels. I wanted to put the kibosh on. You found him?"

He must have been trying out a new cologne. I had the presence of mind not to tell him he smelled like Suzi's Chanel No. 5. Mrs. Wade's son didn't need any extra holes in his head. "It's all taken care of, Mickey. You won't have any trouble from him from now on."

He put his cards and cigar down. "You sure?"

The stooges looked as dumb and dull as test patterns.

"Sure, I'm sure. Scout's honor." I almost raised my hand and then noticed the thugs' eyes tightening.

Cohen got up, dusted off his trousers, and came at me, chuckling. "You're my favorite peeper, kiddo," he confided, resting a palm on the left cheek of my face. "But you cross me and you're wife's a widow. Get me?"

I backed up a step. "Mickey, I'm not married."

"No, not yet," the Connected man said, "but my spies are everywhere, kiddo. So you'd better watch your step, while you still can. Get me?"

I gave him a "Gotchu."

"Then get outta here."

Again Mrs. Wade's son played it smart and got the hell out of there.

CHAPTER 5

Norman had recently moved into new digs on Elysian Street near the construction site around the old Chavez Ravine. On the way over there, I swung into an alley off Cahuenga and parked. Walking back to the street, I went along the rows of magazines on display at World Book and News and bought the latest copy of *Famous Monsters* as a house-warming present. The stand had been here for years, just south of Hollywood Boulevard, but as I went back to my car, I realized one of those *déjà vu* moments. I knew this alley from somewhere else.

I walked back out to Cahuenga, crossed the street, turned around, and looked west. Yep. Buster Keaton had come running out of that same alley in his 1922 chase movie, *Cops*. Keaton was a favorite of mine from my first

case with Mr. P in the early '50s. I stood there now thinking about cops and crooks and today's meeting with
Mickey Cohen. Crime marched on.

Tooling along Santa Monica Boulevard, I finally
picked up the Hollywood Freeway back toward down-
town Los Angeles. The late afternoon sun had warmed
and thickened the city's smog, but I didn't care. I was
driving a Thunderbird and Sinatra was on the radio singing "High Hopes."

I drove down Boylston, parked behind a Packard
with a faded paint job, and switched off the engine in the
middle of the Chipmunks warbling "Ragtime Cowboy
Joe."

Norman's building was a wooden two-story, almost
a shack from the turn of the century, hunched forward
with a wide porch.

His tiny apartment reminded me of my first hang-out
back when I started living on my own in LA. Both places
were almost as cramped as my current office at the
Brown Derby. Mine had been a single room in a low-rent
hotel at the center of the city, empty of non-essential furniture, with a simple washstand and creaky-spring bed.
I'd taped a sheet of paper to shade the low-watt bulb that
hung from the dingy ceiling.

The interior of Norm's place was brighter and the
opposite—in that it was jammed with boxes of records,
piles of books, stacks of magazines and comics, all mingled with unidentifiable electronic equipment and parts of

TVs, radios, tape recorders, cameras, and, for all I knew, nuclear reactors. Yet, out of all this, had come several useful devices like the phone he had once put in my old car and a pair of tiny, two-way radios. I had to admit that Norman was both the smartest and the most not-with-it guy I knew. All kidding aside about his intellect, he was also the most loyal friend I had, at least on the male side. He respected me almost as much as Number One Son looked up to Charlie Chan. But I had to remind myself not to take advantage of his good nature.

I handed him the monster magazine I'd brought.

"Blue blazes," he said staring at the cover. "Issue number five is out! Bela Lugosi." Then in a thick-tongued accent: "You got some blood for me? Blah?"

I picked up a pair of black-framed sunglasses from a cluttered TV tray. "Hey, Norman, can I have these?" During the drive over, my own pair had slipped down into the bucket seat where I'd sat on them, shattering one lens.

He pulled his head out of the refrigerator and winced in the direction of my voice. A lock of dark hair hung over his own thick specs, so I held the pair of shades higher.

"Oh, no. They're not ready yet," he said, bending back to the fridge. "I'm still working on their gain."

The temples of the sunglasses felt thick and heavy. "What's wrong with them?"

He stepped over a cascading pile of LPs, an open bottle of Pepsi in each fist. "Nothing wrong. I'm just putting a mini-radio in them. See? It'll be like a walkie-talkie, but nobody will notice when you transmit and receive signals."

I set the glasses down carefully and accepted a cold bottle of pop.

Norm smiled. "If you added a cowboy hat, you'd have a great disguise as a Texan tourist."

I returned his smile, weakly. "That reminds me. I've got one for you."

He stepped back as if I were about to toss him a medicine ball. "Lemme have it."

I said, "'I'm a cowboy who never saw a cow. Never roped a steer, 'cause I don't know how.'"

He quickly finished the couplet: "And I sure ain't fixing to start in now. Yippie-ki-yo-ki-yay! Okay. Now, I've got one."

I took a long swig, watching his eyes grow eager behind lenses as thick as the bottle in my hand. "Okay, I'm ready. Hit me."

He started in with, "Once she met a deacon and he didn't weaken, but he shouted 'Glory be.'"

This was a tough one, but I was sure that I knew it. "Give me a sec," I said, staring intently at a *Popular Mechanics* mag next to a gutted hi-fi. Then, it came to me. "Now she's going to meet a parson. Have a fifty-cent cigar, son."

Norm nodded with gusto and we both sang, "She's arriving on the 10:10 from Ten-Ten-Tennessee-e."

Cheered by this foolishness, I decided this was the truest definition I knew of friendship.

"Wow." Norm laughed. "I almost said Great Ganymede."

Well, even the best definition of friendship has a limit. "We talked about that, remember?" I told him. "No more ganymedes or jumping blue blazes."

He nodded and burped soda. "Have you seen the new comic strip, *Sky Masters*? It's all about space exploration and drawn by the artist who was doing the *Challengers of the Unknown* comic." He held up the comic page from yesterday's newspaper.

I glanced where he pointed, but tried to appear disinterested. "The art is sort of crude and lumpy—"

Once Norm got going, he was hard to stop. "I've got some more of his work here somewhere in *The Fly*." He cast around the room's assembled mess. "Jack Kirby. Jack Kirby."

I gave him a stage sigh. "Norman, you can show me later, okay? I need to hear what happened with that impersonator guy, Goshwin, I assigned you to follow."

"Gorshin." He looked up, correcting me. "Frank Gorshin, Mr. Wade. Turns out he was right. Somebody *was* impersonating him. I found out that he's up for a role in a Judy Holliday movie. Seems some other guy wanted the part in *The Bells are Ringing*. A friend of Dean Martin's. So the other guy went to the audition in Groshin's place. Later, when the real Frank Gorshin showed up—"

"Let me guess," I said. "The casting director didn't bother correcting the mistake and sent him packing." It had happened before to another actor I knew who tried to steal a role in a Brando picture. There were sleazy agents who would do anything to get their sleazy clients a big break. "So, what was the deal about the bank robbery, Gorshin mentioned?"

"Oh, there doesn't seem to be anything to that at all. I think Mr. Gorshin made it up to dramatically capture your interest and get you to hurry up with his case."

That had happened before, too. "Well, we need to be sure. Nice work, Norman. You're showing real promise as an investigator."

"It helps me with ideas for my novel, too," he said. "Do you want to read my—"

"Not right now, thanks. But you're doing great. Keep at it. Maybe I can set up an office for you at Suzi's agency."

"Swell! Does she have an intercom?"

I was stumped. "I don't really know, but if not, I'll bet you could build one."

We both laughed, even though what I'd said wasn't really funny.

He drank some Pepsi and looked around for a place to set the bottle. "I can't believe I have so much stuff. I've collected a lot of memories." He picked up a copy of *Galaxy Magazine* and gazed at the cover as if it told his life story.

I finished my Pepsi and set the empty on the floor beside the guts of what I took to be a Geiger counter.

I was checking the time on my brother's watch when he asked, "Know what my favorite TV show was when I was eleven years old?"

I heard a siren faintly pass in the distance out on the street.

"It was *Watch, Mr. Wizard*," my friend confessed.

"Not surprising," I admitted. "Funny how stuff like that makes a difference when you're growing up."

"What was your favorite at that age, Mr. Wade.?"

I thought for a moment and then said, "It wasn't a TV show. Not really a movie either. It was a weekly serial from Republic Studios.

The rough and tumble fights were staged and performed by Dave Sharpe. That's why I later became an understudy stuntman."

"Kinda like me, huh?"

I thought for another moment. "You're right. I was eleven years old in 1941. Josh had already joined the Army Air Corp. I used to go every Saturday to the Jewel theatre with a gang from down the street to see the Durango Kid, or Hopalong Cassidy shoot and rope and fight the bad guys."

"You liked cowboys when you were a kid," Norm said. "Not detective movies?"

"No, that came later," I realized. "But I really liked the crime-fighters in the serials. They drove fast cars, jumped off buildings, and pounded fists into the faces of WWII saboteurs."

Norm's mind had moved to a new topic. He was gesturing at the telephone as I said to no one but myself, "Spy Smasher."

"Get a load of what I finished building yesterday," he called.

I drifted over to where he stood next to a table attached to a floor lamp. There was a small tape recorder with a relay switch and bundle of wires beside the phone.

"It's an answering machine."

I waited for more explanation, still half mesmerized by my earlier thoughts.

"A call comes in and this little armature picks up the receiver. Then, a tape plays my voice to the caller. Listen."

The reel of tape spun and Norman's voice came from a tiny speaker near the telephone. "Hello. This is Norman Weirick. I'm not all here. Please speak clearly after I stop talking to record your message to me so I can play it back later and return your call. Bye for now."

"Neato, huh?" the real Norman asked. "After that, it tapes the caller's voice, so I can play it back later."

"Sounds pretty complex," I responded and his face dropped. "But, it might be…great for use in…gathering evidence for a court of law."

That brought his smile back.

I again checked my watch on its Twist-O-Flex band,

this time making more of a show of the action. I told him it was getting late and I had to be shoving off. He waved me out, going back to the tape recorder while cleaning his glasses with a blue tissue that popped up from a Kleenex box.

After another stirring episode with Norman, I usually needed to calm my wits, so I paused on the porch to enjoy the quiet night air. I stopped humming "Ten-Ten-Tennessee" when a white and maroon Edsel cruised slowly past my Thunderbird, with a guy on the passenger side looking into my car. Then the Ford sped past a *STOP* sign and moved into the darkness beyond Elysian.

I caught myself running the side of my thumb back and forth across my lips.

The Noir Man whispered, '*Jumping blue blazes.*'

c/oc/o

I checked under the hood and chassis again, using the flame of my courtesy lighter and the faint glow of a distant street lamp. All seemed safe. *Poor Max. There but the grace of God.*

I held my breath and turned ignition key. The starter caught and the big V8 came alive in my hands, making me feel the way Chuck Heston had looked during his chariot race in *Ben Hur.*

I paused for the *STOP* sign at the end of the street and then eased forward. They must have been parked on a side street, watching. I had to decide quickly how to play this. I didn't know if I wanted to pull over right now and confront them on a city street, or if I wanted to try and be more devious.

The Noir Man said devious was better. I could probably outrun them, but I wanted a terrain-friendly spot where I could obtain a tactical advantage. I accelerated up a hill and saw the Edsel move up fast and slam into my back left bumper, which spun my car onto the shoulder.

I executed a full 180 and took a left onto Park Drive. The russet and white car followed me around the curve. I spun the steering wheel again like a phone dial and the T-bird squealed around another corner.

Coming out of the turn, I stomped the gas and the car leaped forward in a neck-wrenching surge. Through the side-view mirror, I saw the lemon-sucking front of the two-tone swing up, as if to pass.

I hadn't yet learned how to control this beast and my turns kept going wide and off the road.

Somehow, we were roaring down an open dirt road in the middle of the city. I realized we'd spun onto the part of Elysian that was being leveled and graded to make way for the new Dodger Stadium. Since the top was down on the convertible, dense clouds of dust clogged my eyes and throat.

My headlights caught a construction trailer and dormant road-grading equipment to my left. High mounds of earth rose up to the right. The ballpark and its accompanying parking lots would fill more than two square miles when completed. Right now, it was a massive dusty crater of dirt surrounded by access roads for use during the day by steam shovels and dump trucks. In the obscured moonlight, the Edsel cut in front of my grill and hit its brakes with a banshee scream, trying to impact my engine with its wide trunk.

I swung the wheel hard to the right and bounced over a deep rut onto a one-lane, blaring my horn. The two men in the other car weren't apologetic or frightened. They were coming around to a position where the passenger could lean out and aim something dark and ugly in my direction.

I was not ready for gunplay. I punched the button on the dash that automatically released the lock on the trunk. The lid sprang up just in time to provide enough shielding to deflect the two bullets that wanged there.

I could have shot back with my .38, if I had my .38. I ducked low in the seat, wishing someone would stop saying, "Holy shit." The back of my head itched, but no more shots came to scratch it.

I tested the shocks and suspension of the Bird by taking it up and over a mound of soft dirt for a last chance of reaching one of the access roads.

Stomping on the brakes to avoid going over a cliff in the dark, I almost burst head-first through the windshield.

My rear wheels spun in loss sand. "Please don't get stuck here," I told the V8.

I shifted into reverse when pair of high beams careened up and out from the dust with a roar like an Atlas rocket aimed horizontally for my head.

CHAPTER 6

I wrenched the wheel over again, past a sleeping bull-dozer, and almost rolled helplessly down an incline to the center of the huge construction site. There were a couple of bright lights down there and some movement. I recalled reading that the stadium's construction was being filmed for a documentary, but I wasn't sure I'd make it to them, or if I even I wanted to.

What I desperately wanted was a way out, but the narrow dirt and gravel roadway gave me no chance to turn away. The Edsel behind me tried a new tactic of pushing me forward at a speed that felt like fifty miles per second. If I hit the brakes now, I'd skid out of control down the steep precipice, tumbling off the crater's edge.

Over the gunning of the Edsel's engine, I heard a new sound. A rhythmic thumping, like elevated kettle drums. From out of the sky, a searchlight swept past my windshield. The bright blade of light from the heavens sliced through the thickening dust cloud as a helicopter swung past overhead.

It must have come from the lighted area and was now hovering and swooping past with an ear-pounding growl, like a giant attacking hornet.

I stepped on the gas and lost sight of the Edsel while fish-tailing to the bottom of the enormous pit. The chopper darted up the ridge and then circled back in a wide banking turn. Its runners touched down within a dozen feet of the front of my car, and the whirling rotors slowed their cadence. I knew that the police had started using helicopters to monitor traffic on the freeways, but didn't think they had them flying security around construction sites.

A bent figure jumped out of the chopper's bubble, and veered in my direction as the sound of the spinning blades softened to a thousand decibels. "What was that all about?" the man shouted. "Are you all right?"

I coughed away a mouthful of prime LA real estate. "Yeah—thanks to you. Those guys forced me into this pit. Guess they didn't know that you were patrolling here, Officer."

The light around us was still distant and obscure, but I could make out the man's wide forehead and grim expression.

"Not a cop," he said, leaning down to me.

I clinched a fist, while the Noir Man prepared to blast the door open into the guy's hips and torso.

The man looked up at something on the cliff top. "Who was in the other car?

I recalled seeing this guy somewhere before. He had a fair resemblance to Ken Tobey on *Whirlybirds*.

"I'm not exactly certain, but thanks again." I scanned around, but caught no sign of my pursuers.

He batted an open hand at the flying grit. "Didn't you fly with me a couple of months ago?"

I sneezed from the swirling dust and finally placed his face. "Yeah," I replied. "We flew to Vegas together. You'll never get me up in one of those things again."

He snapped his fingers. "Right." Reaching through the window, he said, "Bob Gilbreath of National Helicopter Services."

I unclenched my fist and shook his. "Stan Wade.

"Nice car," he said.

"Yeah, the ads on TV say it's the world's most wanted."

He ran his fingers through his thick hair. "You on official business?"

"Sort of. But I wouldn't still be here without your assist."

"Funny you'd say that," Gilbreath smiled, pointing to the ground. "Your car skidded in right where home plate will be when they finish building the ball field."

It was a perfect straight line, so I said, "Guess that means I'm safe."

We shared a laugh, nervously.

I'd interrupted a second unit shoot here on location, with my own personal chase scene. The crew was filming long-shot footage of the Bell 47J for an upcoming TV episode. Gilbreath's helo was equipped with a radio, so he called dispatch to file a police report. Before the aircraft rose and thrashed away, I asked the pilot not to mention my name. He cocked his head and rubbed a shoulder, but agreed to only report the trespassing incident of a red-and-white Edsel.

෴

For my part, I aimed the car up the shadowed incline and left the gritty world behind. I kept a close eye out for the attacking car as I slowly drove away, eventually following the traffic flowing along the Hollywood Freeway to Cahuenga Pass. I ended up parking the dusty T-bird in the empty lot of a church a block and a half east of Suzi's Spanish hacienda-style apartment house. I hoofed it the rest of the way in the dark and rang the bell at her door. I needed some of her homemade TLC.

When she opened the door, I saw her blonde hair bundled up in a scarf tied haphazardly at the side of her head. One tail of a short-sleeve shirt hung out the front of her blue pedal-pushers. It was one of my shirts. There was a dust-mop in her left hand and tiny beads of sweat on her upper lip. Her coral-blue eyes switched from surprise to mild anger. She actually said, "Eck," and then I kissed her.

After I finished smelling the tang of bleach on the entranceway tiles where she had put me with a hip flip, I hobbled to the low couch that sat in front of her console TV. Red Skelton was clunking around as Freddy the Freeloader, in color.

"What are you doing here at this time of night?" She folded her arms and then unfolded them. "Without giving me some sort of warning."

"Hi, babe. Forgot to tell you. I almost got blown up yesterday."

"Damn," she said. "I'd have paid good money to see that."

My ego and hip were bruised. "I'm not kidding. A federal agent got killed in the explosion."

She stepped over and switched off the TV, serious now. "FBI? Who?"

I told her about Max and the way he'd died.

"That's terrible, Standy." She put down the rag mop and came to sit next to me, giving my cheek a light kiss. "Who did it?"

I decided to let it all out. "Walt thinks it was the brother of that commie-nut who died up in Santa Barbara last summer."

"August Reed, your old duck guy?" I nodded and she

straightened the dust rag on her head and finally removed it. "Why do you believe him?"

"Who?"

"Walt. Why do you believe him when he tells you these things?"

I rubbed my sore hip. "I don't know. Because he's Walt, I guess."

"I always feel that he's not giving you the whole story."

"I have to agree with you there," I said, sharing the details of this evening's car chase and shoot out at Dodger city.

"How do you know they won't come here?" she asked.

"Believe me, I made extra certain I wasn't followed. I even parked in a church lot down the street."

"The Living Hope Fellowship?"

"I guess—"

"That's my church."

"Uh, you have a church?"

She smiled faintly, pretending not to have heard me.

I stretched my arms and back. "Sooo, how goes your puppy-napping investigation?"

"Not nearly as threatening as the one you're working on for Walt. But I may have to go to the dog fights in Tijuana."

"You always get the easy cases," I half complained.

"I'm trying to keep my stress down."

"You'll be out of the country," I reminded her.

"Not a problem," she said. "Travel is good for you."

"As long as someone else foots the bill."

She was quiet for a moment. "I've changed my mind. I think you'd better have a talk with Walt."

Before I could answer, her cat announced his entrance and I immediately protested, "I thought you got rid of that fur-ball."

"He came back. Didn't you, Phooey?"

The yellow tom heard his name and went, "*Murp*?"

I sat up straight in obvious disgust. "You know I'm allergic."

"Why do you think I'm cleaning?"

Phooey jumped into her lap, washed her left ear, and hopped down again to go stretch out under an end-table and thump the floor with its tail.

"You sure that's not a dog?"

"Ha," she said. "Now you're jealous."

"That's poppywash and hogcock. Why do you want me to talk to Walt? I thought you just said you didn't trust him."

"I'm still not sure that I do, but you should at least warn him about what happened tonight. You want to do the right thing, right?"

"I'm not so sure this time—"

"You have to, Standy. For your sake and maybe his, too. It's who you are."

Her earnestness caught me off guard. "You're talking mighty strange lately, little lady."

I watched her try to decide something. At last she got up and pivoted on one flat-sole shoe, announcing, "I need a shower."

Without a thought, I said, "I'll join you."

She began to loosen my belt buckle while nuzzling my neck and we were thus joined the rest of the night.

cɔeɔ

"Hurry up," she called, with surprising urgency. "I want you ready to go when I am."

Forking scrambled eggs and catsup into my mouth, I snickered, "That's what you said last night, too." I sat at the chrome and Formica table in my socks and shorts, eating the breakfast she'd prepared and watching a rosy sunrise through her kitchen window.

She came in, pinning a silver broche to the left shoulder of her Sunday-go-to-meeting outfit. She was even wearing dainty white gloves and a pill-boxy hat.

I heard myself swallow loudly. "We going some-where?"

"You have to get your car."

A ten-watt light came on in my head. "Oh, no—"

"Come on," she ordered, looking at her silver sliver wristwatch. "We'll be late."

I'd already shaved, so it only took a few minutes for her to force me into a fresh shirt, suit, and midnight blue tie before we were out the door, walking down the sidewalk. As we approached the non-denominational church, where my car sat among half a hundred others, I thought desperately for one last reason not to go inside.

"This is against my religion."

She steered my forearm toward the entrance. "You have no religion."

As we climbed the stone steps, I heard an off-key piano and people wailing inside.

The Noir Man said, '*Listen. They're being eaten alive!*'

Suzi lead me toward the altar to sit in the sixth row on the right. I clinched my jaw. Why was I fighting this? What was I afraid of? I took a deep breath and tried to slow my heartbeat.

There was more singing. Then scripture reading.

I turned to look at Suzi's face.

She winked at me.

A white-haired, thin man with a sash around the neck of his flowing dark robe gave us all a sermon about the coming of fall season. The old guy managed to blend in a reference to another fall and then joyfully told the congregation about the joy of redemption.

As a group, we rose and sang again and read some lines from the litany book, or whatever it's called.

When the plate was passed, I opened my wallet and paused. It had been a long time since I'd been to church—ever since my parent's passing. That's what I'd been afraid of, I realized. I took out all the paper money I had and laid it in the plate. Suzi all but suppressed a smile.

Then we sat quietly together with the piano playing a tune I'd long forgotten. During the silent part of the prayer ceremony, I thought about sparing Suzi and others from the kind of trials I'd lived through—that somehow the price I'd paid in losing my parents, my brother, and now Max would balance the equation in my friend's favor.

Suzi leaned toward me and whispered, "This is where we'll have our wedding soon."

"I kinda figured that out," I mumbled back, "'cause I'm a detective."

Soon the music grew louder and we were walking out, shaking hands and chatting with friendly folk whom I'd never met before. On the stroll past my car, heading back to her apartment, Suzi opened her little pocketbook. "Here, you'll need this." She handed me two twenties, folded to the size of a matchbook.

Once safely back inside her place, I used the princess phone to call Walt's office, but it being Sunday, he wasn't there. The person who was, however, said he'd gone up to something called Golden Oak Ranch and gave me directions. At further urgings from Suzi, I decided I should go there and warn him of latest developments.

I kissed my girl goodbye and promised to meet her that evening at the Blue Phrog, a special bar and grill that we favored. I caught myself whistling a hymn off key, as I walked back to my car, checked it for tampering, and drove over to Highland Avenue to catch the Hollywood, Ventura, and then Golden State freeways. I had a lot of driving and thinking to do.

Thank God, it was a nice day.

CHAPTER 7

Riding with the top down under a light blue sky did wonders for my sinuses. Soft, cushiony clouds drifted off to the west. Someday, I'd have to see a doctor about my allergies, or start daily use of those four-way cold tablets. But not today, thank you. The air was clear and so was I.

I drove north on US Route 5 and took the Sierra Highway through Antelope Valley. Usually I hated driving in California traffic, but right now, in this car—it was a true joy ride. I nudged my Thunderbird up past sixty-five mph and enjoyed the wind in my hair, until I discovered that I was lost.

I pulled to a stop at an Esso service station to get directions and a full tank of regular. The attendant wanted to check the oil, water, and air. While he washed the windshield, I learned that he "ain't never heard of a ranch called Golden Oak." An older guy with an unkempt goatee at the next pump overheard our conversation. He filled me in on how to get to the ranch, before driving off in a genuine Ford Country Squire Woodie, which I almost would have traded him even for.

Minutes later, I was streaming like an ocean liner in calm open seas along the freeway and even the rough roads that skirted the Angeles National Forest until I reached Placerita Canyon Road. Ah, the luxury of a fine American automobile. But without any sunglasses, the harsh light began flashing in my eyes. I flipped down the sun visor to dampen the glare and my mind went back to the last time I knew that the Mob had manipulated the movies and the general public.

The average American had no idea that, only a year earlier, organized crime had put the kibosh—to use Mickey's phrase—on Paramount's "Road to Hollywood." The studio was about to begin shooting the Hope/Crosby comedy when word got out that the villains in the script were gangsters infiltrating the motion picture industry. Production immediately came to halt and never started again.

Crosby was busy with his new family and Hope was having trouble with his left eye requiring surgery, so neither star felt compelled to protest loudly. Dorothy Lamour, however, was already counting on receiving payment for her part in the film and had hired me to gather evidence so her lawyers could file suit against the studio. As it turned out, Paramount paid her off and she backed down, but the movie was shelved and the reason was pretty much the same as in Fleming's case: publicity-shy mobsters.

A bank of thick clouds drifted in front of the sun and I could again comfortably see down the road without squinting. I spotted the ranch's entrance with its over-arching sign, made a slow turn, and followed a curving dirt road to a cluster of gray buildings and white fenced-in corrals.

On first impression, the Golden Oak Ranch took me back to my youth. The sprawling hills and pastures with more than a dozen horses roaming free reminded me of the Riding, Roping, and Relaxing Ranch that I used to visit during the summers after World War II. My parents sent me there to "find myself" among the other teens at the dude ranch, who crowded the bunkhouse and stuffed themselves with fried chicken, mounds of buttered mashed potatoes, and thick slabs of hot apple pie.

I suddenly realized that I'd just made myself hungry and involuntarily burped.

I parked the Thunderbird under a shade tree and hoped the real birds didn't spot it. Pausing to scan the landscape, I caught myself smiling. I'd met Suzi for the first time in a place like this. She was wrestling a calf in a corral like the one over by that huge red barn where Un-cle Walt was now coming into view. He had on blue jeans with rolled cuffs and a plaid, open-collar shirt, smoking and walking and arguing with someone about something. A wide-brimmed western hat shaded his lined features and angry expression.

"Look, Charlie," he said, gesturing with his cigarette, "I didn't buy this place for my health. Get those expensive lights trucked up here pronto. We'll need them when the circus vans arrive."

Charlie wasn't happy, but he nodded and hustled off to do as he'd been told. From past experience, I knew that Walt usually got what he wanted.

I caught his eye and ambled over to where he stood fanning himself with his Stetson.

"'Lo, Stan," he said. "Good to see you." A slight breeze caught his hair and made it dance, as his arm and hat rose to encompass our surroundings. "What do you think of her?

I studied the horizon. "I think maybe I should sell my boat and move up here where it's quiet and peaceable."

A rooster crowed ten feet behind us, making my last word ironic.

Walt hitched up his belt, saying, "Glad to hear it," in his nasally, mid-western voice. "I've got good news. The word is Reed's brother, Nickolas, has lit out for the territories. He must have felt the heat bearing down and decided to go underground while he could."

"I'm not so sure about that," I allowed. "I was attacked again last night."

Walt wanted to know the few details I could provide, while he chain-lit a fresh cigarette from the butt in his hand.

"So, even if Nickolas Reed has backed away," I explained, "he still might have left an open contract out on either of us. Which is why I drove up here. You need to be extra careful."

His face hardened at the thought. "So do you. In fact, it might be a good idea if you were to go off somewhere until it's safe."

"Max's death sort of rocked me," I confessed. "I can't help feeling that it could, or even should, have been me who died. I want to be here for his funeral."

"Sorry about that, but his family is having his remains shipped back to South Carolina." He took a vicious inhale from his smoke. "You know, Stan, you can't always pay people back for what happens. Sometimes, the best you can do is pass it forward."

I tried to think of a good way to get out of this conversation. And then Walt gave me one.

"So, have you met with Fleming? I hear that he's leaving for his place in Jamaica tomorrow. Perhaps you and your lady-friend would like a vacation. I could arrange the airfare."

"You're right," I said. "I have talked to my 'friends' to get them to lay off, but I don't trust Cohen to back down so easily."

The filmmaker took another deep drag. "I'd like you

to continue acting as my special agent with Fleming."

"Is there some connection between the two of you that I should know more about?"

He dropped his smoke and stepped on it. "How about this? You do what you can to keep his back safe and *my* 'friends' will do what they can to keep yours safe from Reed."

"Still not sure yet," I answered. "Do you have a phone here?"

He looked at me. "This is not the Wild West, pilgrim. Come."

I followed him inside the main ranch house where I found a modern, professional office and two matronly women typing on noisy Underwoods. Walt pointed to a bank of phones and then wandered off while I called the Biltmore. When Fleming came on the line, I gave him an update. He thanked me and admitted that he still felt threatened, adding, "I don't believe that I shall feel fully relieved until I leave the country."

"I understand that you're flying out tomorrow. Do you think you'd like me to come along with a friend as company?"

He only took a second to reply that this was an excellent idea.

"It's not mine," I said. "It was proposed by our mutual friend."

"Ah. Well, thank him for me, if you get the chance."

When I hung up, I found Walt standing on the other

side of the desk, holding the wallet of FBI credentials and another thin blue booklet. I flipped through the passport, resisting the urge to ask if my eyes were really brown.

"You think of everything," I said, slipping the two documents into my pocket.

"I try."

The Noir Man said, '*Say it, stupid.*'

So I said, "We all try. You succeed."

Walt missed the reference due to a harsh coughing fit. He stabbed out his cigarette in a ceramic ashtray. Once he settled down, I told him, "Those things will eventually kill you."

"Chesterfields? They're mild and outstanding."

"Uh-huh. And deadly."

We walked outside again toward a short young man who'd just come out of the bunk house.

"I'm told," Walt said, waving his cowboy hat at a fat horsefly, "that the real danger is in my house at Holmby Hills and its asbestos ceilings. But life's too short to worry about fantastic theories like that."

"And getting shorter all the time."

He pointed to the approaching kid. "I'm going to put Kevin in a new live-action picture, *Toby Tyler*. Film him and the circus right here along with a batch of other projects I have in mind."

Another Toby, I thought. Lot of that going around lately.

The kid came up, greeted Walt, and looked at me. I

recognized the older version of "Moochie" that Walt had created for the actor, Kevin Corcorin.

Walt asked the kid, "Have you read the new script, Toby?"

"Goin' over it this evening, sir, when I get home," the teen said. "Nice place you got here."

We all looked around and nodded. I coughed lightly and Walt caught on, realizing he hadn't introduced us.

"Stan Wade?" Kevin said, screwing up his forehead. "Baseball player?"

I coughed again. "You're probably thinking of Musial."

"Oh, right, right," he said like Ozzie Nelson. "Stan the Man. So what is it you do, Mr. Wade?"

"Whatever Walt pays me to—within reason."

"Yeah, me, too." He grinned and turned to Walt. "Except I'm a little leery about working with monkeys."

The older man patted the kid's shoulder. "It'll be fine. And it's essential to the plot of the picture."

Corcorin shrugged and moved off, saying quietly, "At least it's not rabbits again."

I watched the young actor walk away and asked Walt, "Rabbits?"

"We had him run around with rabbits in *Spin and Marty*," Walt answered, lighting another cigarette. "Turns out they give him a rash. Listen, Stan. I have an important call to make inside. Do you want to come along or wait here?" He gestured at a rough-honed bench under one of the oak trees, but my attention was drawn to another man who was walking slowly toward us.

"You go ahead," I said. "I think I see someone I know." Like Fleming, this guy could have passed as Walt's brother, except he wore a higher forehead and a ragged goatee.

Walt followed the direction of my gaze. "Oh, yes. Talk to John and I'll be right back."

As Walt left, I realized the guy approaching was the same person who'd given me directions at the Esso station. He continued in my direction, extending his hand palm up, which meant he wanted to help me. If it had been palm down, it would have meant he wanted me to help him. And if it had been sideways, we would have just shaken hands. One of those little things you learn while observing people.

I let him help me sit on the bench, before he settled beside me. He spoke in a soft, resonant voice, and I learned he'd been born and raised in Salinas Valley. He was back home again after decades on the east coast to attend the funeral of an old friend. I looked off as he continued his rambling tale of youth and travels. A couple of red squirrels chased each other around and up the trunk of a broad shade tree.

I saw Walt start back in our direction, and so did the guy next to me. He got to his feet, ran a hand over his thinning hair, and went off without another word.

"Tell me," Walt said, arriving at the bench, "I hear

you plan to marry that girl, Suzi. Are you sure that's the right thing to do?"

I only half heard him. The guy got into the Woodie and put the engine into gear.

"Okay. I'll bite," I said. "Who the heck was that?"

Walt and I watched the car drive off. "Oh, John? He's the quietest loudmouth I know. Told me he planned to write a series of stories, perhaps a novel, of his travels across the country."

"John, who?"

"You didn't recognize Steinbeck? I've known him a couple of years now. Staunch American."

"So, does that mean that he too is an FBI special agent?"

Walt grimaced. "Not everyone I know is in the employ of the federal government."

"Sometimes it seems that way to me. What about Guy Williams?"

Walt increased his grimace. "Please—he's an alien."

"Just asking." Something else he'd said suddenly clicked. "Wait. What do you mean, is marrying Suzi the right thing to do?"

His eyes seemed flinty gray. "I've always thought of you as a sort of lone wolf, Stan. On call, day or night. Your lifestyle isn't conductive to long-term relationships—if you don't mind my saying so." He patted a shirt pocket for his Chesterfields.

I reached over and pulled the pack out for him.

"Yes," I said, crushing it in my hand and letting it drop. "I do mind if you say so."

But during the drive back to LA, the Noir Man kept wondering if Walt knew something about Suzi that I didn't.

CHAPTER 8

It was evening when I pulled into the parking lot outside the Blue Phrog. The sun was a golden beachball floating on the iron-colored surface of the ocean. The last gulls were wheeling around the bar-and-grill's trash bin and other discordant music came from inside the tilted tug here on the shore of Santa Monica.

As I got out of the T-bird, a voice said, "Jeez, Squirrel, that your car? It's two blocks long, not countin' the curb-feelers."

I rotated slightly to show that I hadn't been startled and caught the familiar, loopy grin of Alexia Iglesia. The tough old gal was just climbing off the seat of a cherry-red Indian cycle.

Her hair was short and gray, her eyes encircled by black plastic goggles.

"Howdy, Lex," I greeted her, nodding at the cycle. "Where'd you get the big noise maker?"

She had on a tight pair of Levi's and a jacket with too many zippers. She ambled her weighty frame over in a bow-legged stride that I suspected was exaggerated for effect. Next, she would be spitting tobacco juice at me. Most women her age and recovering from throat cancer would be as soft as a one-minute egg. Lex was the closest thing I knew to hard-boiled. She glared at the trunk of my car. "Are those bullet holes?"

"Tell you all about it—" I said, draping an arm over her low shoulders. "—inside."

We threaded our way past several other cars parked wapper-jawed in the weedy lot.

"Where'd you get the motor-cycle?" I asked, as we started up the wooden ramp to the slanted bar and grill.

"Sonny gave it to me," she said in her gruffest voice.

I held open the door and saw Paul Newman and his wife, Joanne, come out and go past, nodding thanks. A wave of music washed over us as we entered. "He *gave* it to you? Who'd you have to kill?"

"Tell ya all about it—" She smiled. "—inside."

I'd known that smile since our days in the early '50s working together for old Mr. P. It was a smile that would have made Mona Lisa laugh.

"I'd have been here sooner," I said, "but I ran into heavy traffic outside the premier of that *FBI Story* movie over on Melrose."

"That's what ya get for livin' in movieland," she said in her gruffest voice.

Inside, behind the bar, Sonny Goh stood talking with a clutch of customers and freshening their drinks. He was heavily corded more than heavily muscled, with broad plates of pecs visible within his open shirt. A couple of guys in burr haircuts and dark suits and ties were playing darts in the corner. A ceiling fan churned a light breeze of cigarette smoke.

I watched the two guys at the dart board, carefully, and asked Sonny, "How long they been here?"

His puffy eyes narrowed and his petulant mouth said, "Ever since Bennett started his set."

"FBI?"

He shrugged a set of shoulders you could have stacked books on. "IBM. Those finks love lounge acts."

He was probably right, but the Noir Man didn't like it. Sonny Goh had operated the Blue Phrog for over two years, and I'd been coming since it opened. He claimed restaurant and laundry work were still the only two jobs a Japanese could get in America. The Phrog was a forty-year-old tugboat that ran around during a storm back in '56. It rested just above the shoreline, half-tipped, with a solid foundation and fixtures canted at an angle to compensate for the boat's listing to starboard. Tables, chairs, stools, and the long zinc bar that runs fore and aft, all slanted in a way that kept the beer mugs and shot glasses from rolling into your lap. I was sure that a zoning commissioner and a liquor license agent had gotten rich payments from the place.

The hefty barkeep slung a soggy towel over his shoulder and pointed to two empty seats at the far end, near the juke. "Hi, lady." He smiled, looking at Lex, who quickly glanced away.

But I caught it. "Are you kidding me?" I asked. "You two seeing each other?"

Sonny grunted.

"What of it?" Lex asked.

In a way, it made perfect sense. Same age. Same disposition. "Since when?"

"Since none of your beeswax." Sonny crossed his arms and became all chest, forearms, and biceps.

I quickly became interested in the dollar bills that decorated the wall behind him. There was row after row of them, each taped to the wall and signed in black grease pencil by the patrons who'd donated them. One read *Sandy & Doug 25th Anniv.* Another, *Dirty Red Ranch, Texas*, next to *I like Ike*, *Jesus Ate Here*, and *Go Bucks!!*, whatever that meant. There was even a Confederate hundred that read *Georgia Peaches Golf Tour*.

I'd been coming to the Phrog ever since it opened, originally because it was near my boat, but eventually because the sandwiches and live entertainment were generous and inexpensive. Sonny had an in-law in the music industry and a lot of talented singers performed here on the QT when they were in town, as a sort of warm up for their recording sessions. The cramped stage at the stern of the tug had hosted Peggy Lee, Buddy Holly, and, one fabled night, Francis Albert Sinatra. This evening, the crowd got to hear Tony Bennett's mellow tones, live.

I smelled Suzi's spicy French perfume before I saw her. "I can't stand him," she said, coming over to join Lex and me.

"I think he's gorgeous," Lex said.

I gave Suzi's hips a squeeze and whispered in her ear, "Got something important to tell you."

She nudged Lex. "You think anything in trousers is gorgeous. Bennett always sounds off key to me. And look at that nose. You could hang a gallon bucket of paint on it."

We all peered through the accumulating cloud of tobacco smoke, trying to imagine such a scene.

"Ya know," Lex said, "I had a friend who saved three thousand Raleigh coupons."

I had to ask, "What'd he get for them?"

"Three cartons of Chesterfields," Lex answered with a straight face. "And a cough ya could use as a duck call."

I stifled a laugh, and a cough. "Someday they'll outlaw cigarettes."

"Then butt-leggers will smuggle them across the border," Suzi said, accepting my seat at the bar as Bennett's song ended and he took five to moderate applause. "What's the important news?"

I was feeling good, so I shouted, "Drinks on the boat!"

Both women gave me the fish eye. Everyone else cheered thanks.

"Just because I don't imbibe any longer," I explained, "doesn't mean I couldn't buy someone a beer or whisky."

"Someone?" Suzi asked as the crowd roared around us. "How about everyone? And who's going to pay?"

"You're in my church now." I smiled. "I'm passing the offering plate to you."

Lex gurgled a" "Shit fire!" while Sonny called out to me, "What are you drinking, Stan?"

"Something young and fair and debonair."

"Gotcha," he answered and slid an iced Pepsi down the bar.

From the edge of my eye, I caught sight of Norman coming out of the Buoys room. On a whim, I asked the two women, "What's your favorite movie?"

"*Roman Holiday*," Suzi quickly replied, which caused my eyebrows to climb.

"Kate Hepburn?" Lex asked. "Now there's something in trousers for ya."

Suzi corrected, "It was Audrey Hepburn." She sipped smugly from a glass of white wine. "Not Kate."

Lex ignored her. "My favorite's *Mr. Roberts* with Fonda, Powell, and that new guy, Jack Lemmon."

My eyebrows almost crawled off my head.

"Yeah, I know," Suzi said a little cattily. "They're all gorgeous. How do you feel about the Marx Brothers?"

Norman finally arrived through the crowd at an angle. "Hi, all." A ballpoint pen had leaked into his shirt pocket. "Did someone offer free drinks?"

The five of us partied together for another hour or so. Sonny served me a hot dog as tough as a stale tootsie-roll. Bennett sang two more sets. The guy just wouldn't quit. I finally got a chance to tell Suzi about our trip to Jamaica. Unfortunately, I failed to anticipate her reaction.

She looked stonily into my eyes and said, "In the morning? Are you out of your mind?"

I slipped the flats of my hands into my back pockets. "Why not? We won't be gone that long."

She cast around for intelligent sympathy. "I can't just drop everything and go off to the Caribbean."

"I can," Norman said.

"Surely, your dog-napping case can wait a few days," I reasoned. "It'll be good to get away."

"I—I don't have an up-to-date passport," she said, looking down.

"I do," Norman said.

I decided to screen-test her hesitance. "Tell me. What's the real reason?"

Something in his face slipped for an instant and then she said, "No particular reason. I just don't want to go."

"I do," Norman said.

"Yes," Suzi said. "You should take Norman. He needs the experience."

The music was starting up again and the crowd noise rose from the tilted tables. I studied Suzi, who smiled up at me and clinked her wine glass against my pop bottle. "Deal?" she asked.

I saw Norman nodding. Lex and Sonny waited for my reaction. What had I done now? "Okay," I said, taking a deep breath and then a swig of Pepsi. "If that's what you want." The Noir Man remembered Walt's words about Suzi.

"I need to get home and pack," Norm said.

"I'll take you," Suzi offered, setting her glass down on the bar.

Something was definitely off here, but this was not the time and place to get it on.

"You probably need to pack, too," Suzi said, giving the corner of my mouth a peck and my shoulder a small pat. "I'll catch up with you later."

They left together in her Renault under the high moon. I went back to the *Cervantes II* alone, trying not to ponder why I was being avoided.

But I kept boomeranging back to the thought I'd had days earlier. Sometimes people tell you the damnedest things, hoping you'll believe them.

PART II
GOLDENEYE

CHAPTER 9

Betty Boop walked into my dream, carrying a little white puppy. The black-and-white baggy clown did a backward summersault and landed next to a cricket wearing a top hat and reading glasses. The cricket pointed at me with a lit cigarette. Suzi dashed in behind Betty. The two of them looked directly at me and started playing a rapid game of patty cake. Then the clown stepped forward, gave me the finger, and I woke up.

I hadn't had dreams like that for several months. Usually, I could sort of control them, but this time all the characters seemed determined and hostile. Maybe I should have analyzed it more, but I put it behind me and got up from my berth to pack for the trip.

I stuffed extra clothes and toiletries into a scuffed,

brown suitcase I'd used for years since I was a kid. Under the circumstances, I thought hard about packing my .38 as well. The Noir Man was for it, but I finally decided against it, since I'd be traveling through customs. With the current favorable rate of exchange for the US dollar, I could probably buy another handgun cheap in a foreign country.

A foreign country. That sounded...well, almost as strange as my dream. I'd never gone beyond the borders before, unless you counted a few brief trips to northern Mexico. But it seemed like everybody had done it by the time they were old enough to drink anything stronger than 3.2 beer. Going to Jamaica was kind of exciting—but no big deal, right? How foreign could it be? Wouldn't it just be like Tijuana, only floating free in the blue Caribbean? Guess I'd find out soon enough.

Before hitting the airport, I had a couple of stops to make. I picked up a sleepy-eyed Norman, who totted a fat gym bag by its worn straps and a multi-pocketed work vest. His hair was every-which-way, still, with sleep, but he too started to show the unsuppressed anticipation of world travel. He'd made coffee and handed me a paper cup full of the worst brew I'd ever swallowed. Fortunately, our next stop was at the Brown Derby, so I got something that tasted like real java while I left word that I'd be unavailable for the next week or so.

Cindy was already in her office, cranking an adding machine. She gave me a "Hi, Stan" and a few accumulated phone messages, which included nothing that couldn't wait. I'd call Darren McGavin's assistant when I got back and find out what the excitable actor wanted this time.

"Oh, and Mr. Cobb still needs to see you post haste," Cindy said, shaking out a couple of Chiclets and popping then into her lovely mouth. "He's fit to be tied."

I tried to imagine that and told her I couldn't wait, since my plane was scheduled to take off in an hour.

"All right." She chewed. "But he's threatening to toss your office stuff into the street, if you don't shape up. His words, honest."

"I'll have to chance it," I said, transferring a wad of folding money from my cashbox to my coat pocket. "Can you cover for me?"

"I'll try, Stan, but—"

"You're a doll, doll." I bent to plant a kiss on her forehead and that's when I heard Cobb holler my name. "Gotta go."

I left my classy chariot locked in the parking lot and Norm and I caught a cab to the LA International Airport. Inside the busy and oddly echoing building, we showed our passports and picked up tickets for Flight 75 to Miami, with connections to Kingston, Jamaica. I checked my bag, but Norm kept his as carryon luggage.

At a newsstand, I bought a morning paper and a copy of *Time Magazine*. Norm bought a Payday candy bar and the latest issue of *Galaxy Digest*. He asked if they gave Green Stamps, but I was pretty sure he was kidding.

We finally met up with Fleming out on the tarmac, waiting with the other passengers as the gleaming Boeing 707 taxied to the boarding ramp. Our plane was a four-engine jet job, as long as two railroad cars and twice as high. After I quickly introduced Norm to Fleming, we climbed the metal stairs and were greeted by a dark-eyed, brunette stewardess in heels and a snug blue uniform and cap.

There was some slight confusion with our seats when it appeared that I was sitting next to Ward Bond, instead of Fleming. After we got it sorted out, I finally buckled in across the aisle from Norman.

"Pretty ironic, isn't it?" Norm asked the writer, who sat to my left. "We're flying with Ward Bond and you write about James Bond."

"Yes, ironic," Fleming sniffed. I could see that his heart wasn't in it.

Undaunted, Norm went on. "I just finished reading *Moonraker*, Mr. Fleming. Can I have your autograph?" He plucked the vomit bag from the back of the seat in front of him and handed it across, smiling.

I successfully swallowed an explosive laugh as the cabin door clamped shut and the plane lurched toward the runway.

My arms and hands began to sweat. Fleming leaned back like the seasoned traveler he was and closed his eyes. Norm leaned over to try and see out the port window. I followed his gaze and, as we rolled past the terminal, I thought I saw Suzi waving from the observation deck. The woman there wore shades and a Dodgers ball cap, so I couldn't be one-hundred percent sure it was my lady.

There was a groaning turn and a pause in our forward motion and then the pilot brought the turbos to a banshee scream and released the brakes with a jerk. While I tried to concentrate on my copy of *Time*, we hurtled down the runway and jumped quick into an easy climb that briefly put my stomach into free fall.

Khrushchev's pudgy mug was on the magazine's cover. *Explorer VI* was revealing an intense belt of radiation around the Earth. Arlene Francis was taking over the Jack Paar show for a week and her first guest would be the French actress, Simone Signoret.

Norm appeared to be deeply involved in a book entitled, *The Pirates of Shan*. Fleming hadn't changed position. Could he be dead? Then he yawned. So did I, and my ears popped. I switched to reading the newspaper, casual as a snake-charmer, while the plane banked to the east.

Bright sunlight slid across the sports page. The Dodgers were going to play the Braves in Milwaukee later that day for the National League pennant. The new Philip Marlowe series would debut that night on ABC-TV. Over in the comics, Pat Ryan crossed verbal swords with the Dragon Lady again, but I knew she was nuts about him. Had been for years.

The scream of the jets died down into a soothing, low-pitched whistle and we were told we could unfasten our seat belts but not get up yet.

I wanted to stretch my legs, just on principle. Almost everybody, except Norm and me, fired up a cigarette. The stews came around and took drink orders. I popped my ears again, trying to hear what Norman was saying.

He smiled weakly. "I think I'm going to throw up."

I leaned away as he soiled his autographed sick bag. The stewardess with the dark hair and eyes took the bag and gave him a pill. We all waited.

Outside the window, the shining jigsaw puzzle pieces of the Salton Sea flashed back the glare of the sun as we passed effortlessly over them. I tried to distract Norm from his displeasure by chatting about anything that would interest him, detective work, mostly.

"What was your—" Burp. "—first big case?" he asked.

The flashing reflected light caught my eye again and I thought back to the early 1950s when Buster Keaton had told me that his walk-on in Wilder's *Sunset Boulevard* was "inspired direction."

He'd had no lines, of course, playing cards with the other actors in one brief scene, but that was fine by him, since he was famous for his performances in silent pictures. His talkies were not big hits, but his silent features still charmed audiences around the world. Come to think of it, that was exactly the same attitude as Norma Desmond's line in the script, "It's the pictures that got small."

Keaton told Mr. P and me that he thought Billy Wilder was a true genius. "These German directors have it all over us in America," he said. "Europe is a terrific place to make movies, especially back in the old days when Murnau, Lang, and Pabst were at their heights." Keaton's tired face remained stony. "Billy will go a long way, you watch."

Mr. P tried to bring him back to our immediate problem. "Okay, so Wilder is a genius and a great alibi for you at the time of the murder, but that doesn't mean the cops won't still try and pin it on you, Buster. You and Von Stroheim where the only two people there when the script girl died in the swimming pool."

"Yeah," I added my two cents, "but I don't think she drowned there." I wanted to impress Mr. P. "Those bruises around her neck looked like strangulation to me. Whoever tossed her body into the pool did it to cover up the real cause of death."

Keaton smiled, just a tiny bit.

Mr. P rubbed his left shoulder where he'd been stabbed accidently last month by Basil Rathbone. "You're right, Stan," he said slowly. "You've a real knack for this detective work."

I'm sure I swelled up like a balloon full of self-pride. But I didn't spoil the moment by popping off. Instead, I wandered around to the other side of the pool that Paramount had built here at the Getty mansion near Wilshire Boulevard, rather than Sunset. Wilder had called us in to investigate the unfortunate girl's death, on the QT.

When I'd heard that the case involved Keaton, I begged to be the one to come along instead of Gunther or the big man, Jeremy. I'd seen several of Keaton's early films at USC and he'd become my favorite silent actor. We finally eliminated him as a suspect for the girl's murder, days later, but not before I'd saved Mr. P's brother from being tumbled over the edge of a cliff in Benedict Canyon.

"That's really funny," Norman said, looking less green now. "Around that same time, I saw a different picture that made a lasting impression on me, too. It was John Ford's *Rio Grande*."

My throat was dry, so I signaled the stew for a Coke. They didn't have Pepsi on the plane. "Is that the one where John Wayne says, 'Get it done'?"

Norm nodded. "It's what the British call keeping a stiff upper lip."

Fleming had no comment for that.

I leaned across the aisle. "That race where the riders stand up on the backs of two horses is a US Calvary tradition." A chariot race in flashed across my mind. "I wonder if Yakima staged that race and other stunts in *Ben Hur*? Have to ask him when we get back."

Norm simply said, "Yoh."

Fleming appeared to have been put to sleep by our

movie talk. It wasn't a bad idea, and now that Norm had settled down, I wanted to snooze myself. But the stewardesses came around at that point and brought us a surprisingly tasty lunch of steak, fresh vegetables, and ice cream with brandied apricot sauce. '*No tutti-frutti,*' the Noir Man silently groused.

Fleming and I were famished and enjoyed our heavenly meal. Norm passed, focusing on reading a story called "War Game" in his issue of *Galaxy.* He said it was written by Phil K. Dick. Fleming had never heard of him, but I knew Dick was one of Norm's favorite "sci-fi" writers.

While we finished our dessert, I took the opportunity to talk with the British writer on my left. He said a few things that lead me to believe he was, indeed, more than a simple creator of suspense novels. He'd heard me mention *Ben Hur* earlier and his eyebrows went down now, as if I'd tapped him on the skull when I mentioned the scene where it looked like a stunt man had been trampled.

"It's my understanding, Mr. Wade," he said, fixing another cigarette into his holder, "that a man actually did die during the shooting of that scene."

"That's what it looked like to me in the preview I saw. And you can call me Stan."

He didn't offer for me to call him Ian.

The dark-eyed attendant smiled down. "Anything more for you two gentlemen?"

Both Norman and Fleming declined, but the Brit

went on in hushed tones to advise me that it would be highly embarrassing for America, if the Reds could ever prove that someone indeed died during the filming of a huge, international motion picture.

Upon reflection, it didn't seem to me to be all that serious of a threat, but Fleming was adamant. "Dominoes, Mr. Wade. Dominoes. The East won't wait long before starting the fall."

I said, "Okay," and wondered why I needed to protect such an obviously well-informed and capable man.

Another hour passed while we soared on at near 30,000 feet and I filled the time listening to slow jazz from my seat's stethoscope earphones.

I dozed off once and caught myself wondering again about Walt's "opposite number."

The Noir Man warned, *'There's something he's not telling you. The trouble's just starting.'*

I said, "Shut up."

Norm said, "Were you just talking to me?"

Outside, the sun was setting far behind us in the golden, distant west. And I was journeying farther and farther from home.

CHAPTER 10

The transcontinental flight seemed to go on forever. Finally, around 5 p.m. local time, our plane landed in Miami and Fleming said, "Explain to me again why your friend had to come along."

I was a little irked by this and leaned over to quietly confess, "He's the smartest person I know, Flem. And, besides, he hates commies."

The writer's eyes grew cold from my taunt. "Most amusing," he commented in what must have passed as standard British humor. "Wait until he hears about Castro."

"Last I heard," I said, sort of showing off, "Castro is just a guerrilla rebel who forced the Cuban President into exile months ago. In fact, a respected news source quoted him as not being a Communist."

"We shall see," Fleming said in a way I didn't like.

The Miami International Airport mirrored that of LA. I thought for a minute we'd made an in-air U-turn. The same bustling crowd of passengers and visitors; the same ticket counters and vending areas; the same runways, gates, rows of stiff, uncomfortable chairs; and even a few palm trees, nodding in the breeze.

We located our connecting flight on British West Indies Airways and boarded for takeoff to Kingston in twenty minutes. It was a two hour flight on a Gulfstream twin-engine turbo-prop. There were three other passengers, including someone we all recognized, Boris Karloff.

Living all my life in and around the City of Angels, I'd learned that most movie stars are just exaggerated personalities. Somehow, Karloff transcended all that. Norm was in hog heaven upon seeing the "old chap" again. He'd met him before somehow, during the filming of *Frankenstein 1970* and they chatted briefly before takeoff. Karloff looked to be in his seventies and walked with a cane. "Children adore me," I heard him tell Norm. "They don't have to get undressed for bed at night. I scare the pants off them."

Norm strapped himself back into his seat next to me, all aglow. "Boris is on his way to Porto Rico to do *Arsenic and Old Lace* at the San Juan Drama Festival."

Then, before I was fully prepared for it, we were aloft again, soaring out over the Atlantic in a plane that sounded like a Mixmaster and banked like a rollercoaster.

I could soon see dark spots in the ocean below that were actually the shadows of small clouds above us. I didn't know if I wanted to be higher or lower.

Karloff was seated over my left shoulder. Across the aisle and a couple of seats directly behind me sat a bearded man who had been the first to board. This fellow remained quiet during the first half of the flight, but now moved up the aisle as if searching for his bag in the overhead rack.

One of the stewardesses approached him, just as the plane shook from entering a storm front.

I watched the bearded guy hand her a piece of paper. Her face went white and her eyes searched the folds of his jacket as if to measure him for a gun.

His coat did appear to hang oddly and despite the buffeting of the flight, his right hand never left the jacket pocket.

"Oh, miss," I called, glancing at Norm, who was also studying the situation. He reached into his vest and placed a thin packet the size of a matchbook into my palm—one of his tiny radio transmitters. "Miss?" I called again with more urgency, watching.

"I'll be with you in a moment, sir," she said, eyes still on the bearded guy.

"Don't give me that," I protested, rising from my seat.

Norm popped an earphone into the side of his head.

I came forward, pretending not to notice the stern

look on Bearded Guy's face. "Can't you see that my friend back there needs attention? He suffers from severe air sickness."

Norm moaned on cue.

"Get him a pill or something."

Fleming began to take an interest, along with Karloff farther back in the plane.

"I'm sorry, sir." The stew tried to smile, as I dropped the listening bug into the mouth of her uniform's hip pocket. "You'll have to wait your turn. Now, please return to your seat."

I caught a glimpse of the note clutched in her hand and read a word that chilled me. Bomb.

Bearded Guy and the stew went into the pilot's compartment and closed the door behind them.

Another stewardess, a blonde this time, came forward with a paper cup of water for Norm. He accepted it with a worried smile and asked for more please. The girl went back down the unsteady aisle as I came back to my seat.

Norm listened with one ear and told me. "He wants to go to Cuba. Says the plane can be used to help the rebels."

"That's insane," Fleming contributed. "The rebels have won already in Cuba."

"Hey, I don't write this stuff," Norm said. "He's a fruitcake. Says he has a gun and will use it on the co-pilot."

Outside the aircraft's thin skin, the weather turned rougher.

"We're still in hurricane season," Fleming offered, tightening his seat belt.

I swallowed dryly, ears popping again.

"Something bad is going to happen," Norman warned.

The blonde stew must have had the same idea, because she moved up to the front and watched the closed cockpit door where her co-worker had gone with Bearded Guy.

The plane jumped and tilted through a sudden flash of lightning to our starboard.

I got up, not sure what to do exactly, but wanting to do more than just sit back and *not* enjoy the ride. As I crossed over Norm's feet, he placed a make-shift weapon in my left hand. I looked down at a plastic toy dart with a small red rubber ball stuck on its point.

I gave Norm a questioning look.

"I got it last night at the Phrog," he said.

I gave him another look, the one that said, "We're going to have a serious talk, if we live through this."

He turned a little greener as the plane shook like Don Knotts.

The blonde was about to knock on the cabin door, when she saw me coming toward her. Thunder rumbled all around and the plane bounced like a cork in the ocean of night.

I was starting to feel queasy, but there wasn't time to explain, so I reached out and pinched her hard on the left breast.

She screamed and cursed like a longshoreman, causing the door to bang open.

I pushed her aside and down, breathing, "Sorry, miss."

The plane lurched up and to port. Bearded Guy swiveled a black automatic in my direction. The stew beside him contributed a scream of her own, and I thumbed the rubber ball off the point of the dart and let fly.

Up in the stormy night sky, seventy miles out over the Florida Straits, the dart silently soared and sank deep into Bearded Guy's hand, which opened when he shook it. The gun dropped to the deck while his bomb-laden body fell back on top of the co-pilot and his control panel.

The automatic pistol kicked off the deck and fired, sending a bullet past my right ankle. Someone behind me yelled. Sparks flew up past my eyes as I dove forward, my heart thumping in my chest. The co-pilot was tangled up with Bearded Guy's body and a couple of wires hung from it like dark snakes.

The pilot hunched his shoulders and banked the Gulfstream on a course that promised to put us in the real Gulf.

I wanted to get to that bomb. Bearded's eyes were fierce and locked onto mine.

He plucked the dart from his hand and started to grab at something under his coat.

The stew next to him was still screaming, but she started kicking a pointed shoe at the skyjacker. It wasn't enough to stop him.

I planted a hard right fist into the middle of his "Cuba Libra" exclamation and followed up with two quick lefts, because my left is pitifully weak.

It was enough.

Out of breath, I helped the stew lift Bearded off the co-pilot. Another flash of electricity beyond the windshield joined the sparks coming from under the plane's dials and gauges.

"I don't have control," the pilot shouted.

"My God," the stew shouted back. "We're going down!"

"Get back to your seats and strap in," the pilot ordered loudly.

"And stop shouting," the co-pilot shouted over all of us.

We hustled aft, dragging Bearded by the collar.

The blonde produced a set of handcuffs from somewhere and we belted Bearded's dead weight into a front row seat, hands locked behind him.

"What happened?" Norm, Fleming, and Karloff asked me in overlapping dialogue.

"I'll tell you about it when we land," I said, buckling into my seat.

The aircraft jumped again as the engines whined and rain pelted the windows.

"You mean, *if* we land," Norm said. He turned in his seat. "Mr. Karloff, I just want you to know that it's been an honor—"

"Just. Shut. Up," the old man roared, raising his cane. "Strap in and keep your trap shut."

That's when we both noticed the blood leaking down the left leg of Norman's trousers. Norm noticed it too and immediately conked out.

I didn't know that an unconscious person could still throw up.

The plane continued to be buffeted by the heavy weather. We all hung on. During one slip slide, the fillings in my teeth were nearly rattled loose. We reduced altitude, dropping at one point like a high-speed elevator.

The rain let up and I saw a cluster of trees flash by in the faint moonlight. The airplane came down hard on its tail wheel. The front wheels struck and we bounded high into the air. Fleming's face held the color and sheen of a pearl.

We came down hard again. The right landing strut collapsed and the fuselage scrapped with the sound of a circular saw. The right wingtip dug into the ground. We spun around, rose into the air, and tried to flip over. Norm's book smacked me in the face. Then the left strut snapped.

The plane slid on its belly and came to a stop. Everybody exhaled as our collective adrenalin slowly lowered.

❦❦❦

"I'm awfully sorry," Karloff said, looking up with watery eyes. "I'm the one who should have kept his trap shut."

Norman grinned slightly and shook his head. "Man, that was electric."

We were taxiing to a stop on a well-lit airfield and the winds had died down to a bluster.

Fleming intently stared out the window into the night. "Where are we?" he asked the stewardess whom I had pinched.

"On the ground," she answered, giving me a glare and a wide berth.

"I know that, dammit," he snapped. "Where on the ground is the question? Cuba or Jamaica?"

"It's a naval base. McCalla Field. Guantanamo."

Norm said, "The only McCalla I know is Irish."

"We're you listening?" Fleming said. "We're *not* in Ireland. We're in Cuba."

"Irish McCalla plays *Sheen, Queen of the Jungle* on TV," Norm said, gritting his teeth as we helped him off the plane.

Fleming seemed extremely steamed for a guy who had escaped from being blown to bits in the air. Karloff, on the other hand, was so impressed that he gave Norman his cane, tossing off, "I only need it occasionally when my right knee acts up. I assure you, I'll be fine without it."

It was still raining moderately as we scuttled across the wet airstrip to a dark concrete-block building nested between two larger hangers. Naval officials tended to Norm's wound and questioned the rest of us for over an hour.

The two pilots, stews, and I all told the same series of events.

Bearded's wallet identified him as Jose Rodrigo, a taxi driver from New York City, who wanted to capture the plane for the "glory of the new Cuban nation."

A Navy CPO near me scratched his left ear and grumbled, "This is the first time something like this has ever happened."

"Well, get used to it," Fleming advised. "And you need to start searching passengers for weapons from now on."

"You all were on a British flight," the Chief Petty Officer advised back, shaking his burley head. Then he breathed, "Sombitch douchbag wet backs."

I didn't bother to comment. I was just glad to have a pulse and feel my feet on solid ground.

The Base Commander, Vice Admiral Thomas Curtiss, had been alerted to our unscheduled landing and came over to reconnoiter.

"The real hero," Karloff lisped at him, "is this young man, Norman Weirick."

A corpsman had patched up the meaty portion of Norm's thigh where the stray bullet had grazed it. He'd also shot him full of antibiotics and pain killers.

My own right leg was starting to give me a little trouble. I guess I'd sprained it or something during the violent fight and flight. I felt a deep tweak in the back of my hip every few minutes and noticed that my right fist was a little sore too, but I dismissed it all as the usual cost of doing business and the price of success.

The base commander was impressed with how we'd foiled the hijacking. He tossed Rodrigo into the brig, saying, "You are part of the rebel alliance. Take him away."

Like Norm, Vice Admiral Curtiss had read some of Fleming's books and he recognized Karloff—who wouldn't? So he was delighted to make arrangements for us all to be transported safely to our original destinations, courtesy of the American military.

Norman was a little more out of it than usual. He waved the cane in the air and slurred, "Kid Weirick, Defender of Justice, has a flash once in a while."

"Indeed he does," Karloff confirmed. "Nice work to the both of you."

Norm started singing, "Here I come to save the day. That means that Mighty Mouse is on the way."

"That kid's weird," the CPO said.

Karloff laughed. "Indeed he is."

"I think he's going for an Oscar nom," I told Fleming, who remained stiff lipped with his eyes on the horizon, as if he were waiting for a bus. I was beginning to dislike the writer. Too cold for my taste.

Both the Noir Man and my right leg continued to feel uneasy.

CHAPTER 11

The flight they set up for us was even smaller than the Gulfstream. Neither Norm, Fleming, nor I liked it, but the commander was insistent that we accept his appreciation. So, the next morning, we all balanced our collective weight into single-engine modified Beechcraft Bonanza for a 100 mile hop to the Boscobel Aerodrome in Jamaica. Karloff caught a later, bigger aircraft to Puerto Rico. Lucky fellow.

We only flew for about forty-five minutes and never higher than 3000 feet above the waves. The little plane bobbed along like a happy hummingbird with me in the co-pilot's seat. That's how small it was. I couldn't help remembering that Buddy Holly and Ritchie Valens had crashed and burned in this very type of plane only seven months earlier.

The pilot, a career navy man with twenty years of service, tried to entertain his captive audience with a shouted stream of off-color humor. Norm was doped and out of it all. Fleming stoic. I looked down through the side window only a couple inches from my face and tried to concentrate on the dots of white below us that were minor whitecaps on the dark blue of the eternal sea.

We traveled along like that, buzzing and seemingly skimming, as the island of Jamaica grew fatter and greener on the horizon.

We landed easily on the north coast at an airport the size of a kid's softball field, and only slightly as well maintained. I thanked our pilot and got out, feeling that I'd accomplished something extremely important. I helped Norm to the ground, and we hobbled—him with a crutch and me with the cane—to a two-car garage and attached radio tower surrounded by fuel tanks and a half dozen chickens.

"I never want to watch another episode of *Sky King* as long as I live," Norm confessed, while we filed through customs.

Fleming immediately searched for a taxi, but a five-foot-two, unctuous government official had heard of our situation and already had transportation arranged.

"We have never met, sirs, but it is an honor to serve you, sirs," said Fletcher Cooke of the Royal Jamaican Customs Service. The busy little man ushered us into a waiting red and yellow pre-war Packard and told the driver—the blackest young woman I'd ever seen—to take us to Fleming's estate, Goldeneye, "with immediate haste."

Fleming tried to protest, but our acceleration pushed him back into his seat.

We were soon swerving along a two-lane road in the mid-day sun, and it was so hot I thought I might need a hat, but a hat would only make my head hotter.

Norm read my mind and asked, "Hot enough for you?"

I tried to set fire to his hair with my eyes. I immediately regretted giving him a harsh look. It was hard to act like a normal human being, after all I'd been through in the last twenty-four hours or so, but I tried to change the channel and act in a more friendly mood.

"Maybe we got off on the wrong foot," I told Fleming. "Let's talk. My middle name is Dalmas. What's yours?"

He froze for a second and I almost missed it. "Let's discuss more important matters instead," he said, lighting another of his fancy cigarettes with a jet of flame from butane lighter.

"Good idea. Tell me, what's your favorite movie?"

His eyes were adding and subtracting. I held them with what I thought was an innocent expression, until he said, *Storm Over Asia.*

"Wow," Norman declared, fanning himself with an open palm. "You go back."

Fleming ignored him and asked me, "Do you think the Mob was behind the hijacking?"

I adjusted my right leg to a less painful position. "No, I doubt that they hate you enough to take down an entire airplane."

He seemed to make more mental calculations as we sped down the highway. His complexion reddened and his high forehead began to sweat from more than the heat. "That's good news, I suppose."

I sat back wondering if I'd said something for what seemed like five minutes.

Fleming winced. Then he grimaced and quietly groaned. Clutching at his left side, he bent far forward.

Norm called, "Is—is he having a heart attack?"

I reached out and pulled the writer upright. He gasped out through clinched teeth and cigarette breath, "Get me to a hospital."

I shouted to the driver, "Take us to…hospital, immediately," and the Packard picked up speed.

☙❧☙

Norm and I quietly killed time, seated in a small waiting room of a moderately modern medical clinic, anticipating the return of a doctor with news of Fleming's condition.

I tried to let my mind relax. It had been a hectic couple of days in an extremely busy year. Max had died,

Walt had told me half-truths, my girlfriend was acting weird, and an unknown Red was out to kill me. I'd survived almost being driven off a cliff and nearly blown up in a plane over the Caribbean.

It had been a time for "joyful participation in the sorrows of the workplace," as my old friend, Gunther used to say. I'd been serving others for months now, sort of joyfully, and felt I deserved a little rest. I wanted to unwind the Noir Man and regress until I enjoyed life more.

In some respects, 1959 had also been the best year of my life. Regardless of all the hassles and run-arounds, things were improving. Here I was, I told myself, sitting in a tropical paradise, on a simple assignment with another good friend. I took in a deep breath and let it out slowly. Even my sinuses had cleared. Life was essentially good.

We'd waited here now for nearly an hour. Two Jamaicans, a man and a woman, sat close together against the opposite wall, staring fixedly at Norm and me.

Norman fidgeted with the bandage on his leg. "I've got one for you."

This didn't seem like the best of times, but… "What the hell," I replied. "Shoot."

Norm recited: "Every year at the Met, they go deeper in debt. You would think they were bound to go broke."

The Noir Man said, '*They don't want Pagliacci.*'

I repeated this, adding, "Give them Liberace. That would be a master stroke," and beamed.

Norm nodded and we both sang, "You got to give the people hoke."

The Jamaicans looked at us as if we were loony tunes. I wiped my already soaking handkerchief over my face and smiled at them. They averted their eyes and somehow their act made me feel cooler.

My pal with the grazed leg brought out a waxed paper bundle of Oreo cookies from one of the many pockets of his vest and we munched together waiting for word on Fleming's condition. I offered to share one with the waiting couple, giving them my best smile. They refused the cookie and the smile, probably because of our off-key singing.

Everybody's a critic.

Abruptly, a dark-faced doctor banged into the room through a swinging door and looked in our direction, saying to nobody but himself, "No, no. He is not out here either." He addressed us with an alarmed expression. "I'm sorry, but where is your friend now?"

"Where is—" The rest of the sentence lodged like chicken bone in my throat.

"He's with you," Norm said, starting to get up.

"No, no, no." the doctor said. "I left him in the exam room and he is gone."

"Gone?" I questioned the doctor. "You were supposed to be treating him for a cardiac arrest."

Doctor Nono raised his palms to the heavens. "No. He has vanished. Poof."

დ/ა/ა

"He couldn't have just vanished," I told the police inspector. "Either the Mob or the Reds have got him." The minute I said it, I knew it must have sounded ridiculous, but I figured it might be a good way to get the local constabulary moving in the right direction.

Unfortunately, the stern-faced police captain wasn't budging or buying it. He'd performed a quick search of the premises, quizzed the doctor, and called back to his station with details and a few quick instructions.

Now he was back to questioning Norm and me, while tapping our passports against the palm of his left hand.

"American organized crime has no footing here in Jamaica, as they do in Cuba with all its hotels and casinos," Captain Foster said, with a pained expression. "And the Reds, as you say, do not exist here, as well."

"That's what you think," Norm told him.

The captain went on. "The man you brought to the clinic cannot be located."

"We know that," I said, evenly. "That's why we called you. Ian Fleming has been abducted."

The policeman shook his head. "You were observed by witnesses, babbling like locos. Isn't it more likely that you, yourselves, are the cause of the man's disappearance?"

"Now wait just a cotton-picking minute," the Defender of Justice protested.

"Any delay, Officer, could lead to Fleming's death," I told the captain.

"Ah, I see," he replied, as another man came in the hospital's entrance. "You are threatening me, then?"

"No, no," I quickly amended. "All I meant was that Fleming is out there somewhere and the people who have him could kill him any time."

"What does he mean?" the new man asked. He wore a dark short-sleeved shirt open at the collar, tan slacks, and a concerned look. "Who is this, inspector?"

The Noir Man made me say, "Who the hell are you?"

The captain clutched my arm, tightly. "Be careful, sir," he advised the stranger. "This one is raving and may be dangerous."

The man shook his head and extended his hand, palm sideway. "It's a pleasure to meet you, Mr. Wade."

I had a pretty good idea now who he was.

"This," the captain explained, taking a step back, "*this* is Mr. Fleming."

"Ian Fleming?" Norm said. "For real, Ian Fleming?"

"Yeah," I sighed, swatting a mosquito that had just stung the back of my neck. "I sort of saw it coming." I took the man's hand and we shook. "My middle name is Dalmas. What's yours?"

Without hesitation, he said, "Lancaster."

"What's your favorite movie?"

The real Fleming looked at me oddly and then chuckled. "Anything by Hitchcock, I suppose. Is that the correct counter-sign, Mr. Wade?"

Feeling a little embarrassed, I said, "It does sound like spy stuff, doesn't it? Sorry."

"Not at all."

Captain Foster said, "So I take it that you know these men?"

"In a manner of speaking," Fleming replied. "We have a mutual friend, the Grey Seal, in the States."

I knew that Walt had favored that name once upon a time.

"Ah, I see," the police officer said, handing back our passports. "If Mr. Fleming vouches for you, I can do no more."

"Thank you, Captain Foster." Fleming nodded. "Might I suggest that you send forces out to locate the man who impersonated me?"

"Yes, yes. It will happen at once."

"And tell the doctor that we'll be leaving together in my car."

Captain Foster saluted sharply, clicking his heels in respect, but the soft leather of his boots made almost no sound.

Norman wasn't confused. He just wanted confirmation of this latest craziness. "You mean our Fleming was a phony all along? Was he trying to lure us into something or what?"

On second thought, I guess he was confused. I tried to dope it out. "I only met him a few days ago because Walt sent me to see him. He said he was Fleming and he knew about the Syndicate not liking your books," I told the real Fleming. "He also knew about your place here in Jamaica."

"With a little research, you'll find that's common knowledge," Fleming said, opening a cigarette case.

"There," I pointed. "He even had one of those."

"My boy," the writer replied, "are you certain you are indeed a private inquiry agent?"

I didn't think there was any reason for him to get snotty. I struggled with the heated situation and climate. "I've been a PI for almost a decade, okay? Anyone can be taken in once in a while."

"Yeah," Norm said, "anyone."

"Captain," I said, trying to capture authority. "When we dismissed the taxi that brought us here, we dropped off our luggage in an alcove. The false Fleming's bag should still—"

Everybody rushed to the clinic's entrance. We found the blue Samsonite case containing a 9 mm Luger and a letter to Yuri Kaminski at the Biltmore Hotel, instructing him to "play the long game." It was handwritten on plain paper and signed Nic or Nik in a loose hand. The envelope was post marked three days ago from East Berlin.

Fleming said, "My doppelganger could have started back there by now."

"Or," I said, "he could still be out there waiting."

"In the meantime, could I have your autograph?" Norm said.

CHAPTER 12

Goldeneye, Fleming's modest estate in the town of Oracabessa, only a few miles from the airport, was actually a single-story, white stone hurricane-proof building with a small garden and a smaller access to the turquoises sea.

The cozy two-bedroom structure sat surrounded by lush green bougainvillea bushes and tiny lizards. In the sweltering afternoon, I could smell the jasmine shrubs and hear the crickets zing and the tree-frogs glunk.

We had all piled into Fleming's black Sunbeam Alpine and driven—on the left side of the cactus-lined A3 road—the short distance to this comfortable home. Once there, the author had offered drinks to counter the lack of ocean breeze. The ice in my ginger ale melted almost immediately. In fact, the glass had quickly sweated through its napkin and the moist paper had already started to dry from the heat. I wished I could say the same for my shirt.

Both Norm and I wasted no time getting short, individual showers. We dropped our bags in the guest room and changed into fresh duds, taking care not to irritate our injured limbs. Nonetheless, I attempted to perform a few vaudeville tricks with Karloff's cane and almost broke the ceiling fan.

When we came back into the estate's wide central room, we were greeted by a guest.

"This is Teddy Whiteside." Fleming introduced a wide-shouldered black man with a scruff of salt-and-pepper curl on his round jaw. "He used to own the place."

"Dat was befo it wa called Goldeneye." The Jamaican grinned. "Our famblies go back together a long time." Whiteside held a glass of amber rum in one hand and a thick unlit cigar in the other. He put the cigar down and wiped a massive pale palm on the leg of his pants before shaking hands all around. "Boss Fleming and me are practically related. My momma and him—"

"Let us not go into that now," Fleming warned.

The big dark man dipped his cigar into his rum, but still didn't light it.

Fleming went on. "Teddy manages the local ice plant and could be useful in locating the faux Fleming, if he's still on the island."

The four of us shared information and dinner at a

seafood restaurant on Fisherman's Pier overlooking a small fleet of pirogues and other fishing boats moored in Ocho Rios Bay. I filled the writer in on the situation with the Mob and he said he'd already been thinking about switching the bad guys in his novels to a world-wide corporate terror organization.

"Good," I answered. "Mickey Cohen will appreciate hearing that."

"Who's dis Mickey fella?" Teddy Whiteside asked.

"He's in the machine business," I said dryly. "Vending, slot, and voting machines."

The big man threw back his head and laughed heartily like a black Sidney Greenstreet. Both he and Fleming drank Red Stripe, the local beer, straight from the bottle. Norman tried one and quickly switched to club soda, like me.

"Maybe you'd like a sarsaparilla," I suggested, but Norm misunderstood and protested against any drink called a "sassy gorilla."

After the new laughter died down, we all got down as well, to business.

"I made a call," Teddy said, "and a frend o mine at da Ocean Sands Hotel say he saw da Boss register der dis aftanoon."

"But, of course," Fleming said, "it wasn't me."

I asked, "Where is this hotel?"

"'Bout a kilo from here." Whiteside jerked a thumb over his right shoulder.

"Then let's go before we lose him."

"Dat won be so easy. Dis is the night o the Ska Festival and, if you hadn't already noticed, the whole area is fillin up with revelers."

Norman wanted to know what ska was.

"A new kinda music dat's caught on like lightnin. Combination o jazz an calypso. Very sublime. Everbody on the island is doin it dese days."

"Sounds a little like Mardi Gras," I said, nudging back my chair.

"Da streets will be packed wid bands and crowds o dancers," Whiteside advised, already swaying from side to side from imagined music.

Out in the street, beyond the restaurant, a happy mob had begun to gather in the night, making it seem even hotter. People all around were strolling, biking, laughing, and drinking.

Every so often a firecracker or two would jolt the herd into a nervous surge. And then the ranks would close again and good times rolled on.

I didn't see how we would be able to make it back to Goldeneye, let alone travel to the Ocean Sands Hotel where the imposter had been sighted.

"We'll have to go on foot," Fleming called out above the gathering din.

The horde of partiers continued to grow and mill about us as we pushed our way down Main Street.

Everyone was chatting, chuckling, smoking, and

dancing to the music that pulsated from small bands playing guitars, trumpets, and even bongo drums.

Norm hobbled along, holding tightly to my sleeve. "They're doing everything here, except spinning and twisting."

"Not quite everything," I answered. "But someone will think of that, too. You can be sure."

As we neared the hotel's front porte-cochere, I thought I saw Fleming in a straw hat and blue shirt covered with bright images of red and golden parrots.

In haste, I almost lifted Norm as we rushed forward. Our quarry sighted us, probably because we looked like a bad three-legged race. We dashed ahead, as he scanned to left and right. Then he dove in the direction away from us, through the mass of raucous celebrants.

A five-piece band—piano and all—on a flatbed tractor-trailer circled the square and separated Norm and me from the other two members of our party.

A host of bouncing bodies danced around us, swinging arms in two-four time while drums pounded and a sax wailed in our ears. I caught a glimpse of the blue, yellow, and red shirt edging around the side of a dark, low building.

Someone yelled, "Skavoovie," over a loudspeaker and the audience screamed back the greeting, bobbing to the one-two repeat of the musical beat.

We cleared the corner of the building and found a high, chain-link fence, but no imposter. I thought I could hear running footsteps slapping cement on the other side of the fence.

"Get the police," I shouted to Norman. "I'm going over." He started to limp away and then pointed to a pad-locked gate. "Go now," I hollered and began clawing my way up the side of the fence.

"I'll try and cut him off at the pass," Norm called out.

I came down hard on the concrete yard next to what looked like an ancient warehouse. A single pale light hung over a doorway and faded sign that read, *Sugar Mill Rum*. Heading for the relative safety of the light, I began to hear rushing water over the cheerful, distant crowd noises.

I took two more steps toward the light and saw that the door was labeled *Office*. It was also splintered and ajar. That was when I made the first of about four bad decisions in the next few minutes.

It was as black as the Le Brea Tar Pits inside. I paused for my eyes to adjust, but it was taking too long. I fumbled out my courtesy Zippo and spun the wheel with my thumb for a quick look around. Mistake number two.

The office was deserted for the night. There were wooden desks, chairs and file-cabinets, stacks of papers, a cluttered bulletin board, and an open door off to one side, but no people.

I should have turned around and gone back out into the yard, but that second door beckoned me like a Lorelei into the warehouse proper. Call that mistake number three.

I struck the lighter again and burnt my finger on a spark. I put it out, but the after image in my mind was full of pallets and crates of Jamaican rum in a cavernous vault. I was tempted to call out, "Marco," to see if he'd respond with "Polo." That's when I found I was holding my breath, waiting for some slight sign that would lead me in the right direction. I strained to listen, but only heard the distant roar of rushing water.

I had some loose change in my trouser pocket, but no weapon, which was another mistake. I tossed what few coins I had into the darkness to try and draw him out. They clattered and tinkled into silence. Then I saw a straw hat sail through a ray of faint moonlight over my right shoulder. The imposter must have liked my idea of throwing things in order to confuse or distract.

I realized abruptly that he had to be behind me. I started to duck and turn in the same motion and felt my last mistake slam into the base of my skull. The lights seemed to flash on for a second and then go out completely.

c/oc/o

For a moment, I dreamed of Max. He was chasing a woman I knew, a woman I'd killed. Then someone was slapping my face over and over. In the dim light, it looked like Norman. I came up swatting and tasting dust from the floor.

"He made me do it," Norm shouted, backing away in panic.

I needed a new head, but I doubted they had one my size in all of Ocho Rios. We were being held at gunpoint by Fleming the Fake. I tried to think of his real name. Yuri something. But the pain at the back of my head demanded my full attention. I resisted giving it, offering up my left hand instead, which caused the pain to bit even deeper into the back of my brain.

"Get up, shitheads," our host commanded, waving his revolver at us to show who was boss. "Turn around and lean into that wall."

I rose slowly, winced in Norm's direction, and shuffled around as ordered to face a tall stack of rum crates.

The imposter's voice was as smooth as a shark on ice. "So you finally figured it out, Wade."

At some point while I'd been busy dreaming, a dim electric light had been switched on, creating crazy shadows around us. Or maybe I was still in dreamland. No, I could hear the cascading water nearby, but it wasn't enough to drown out Norm's comment. "I'm sorry, Mr. Wade. I thought I could pick the lock and help, but he caught me like a flatfoot."

"That's flat footed," I corrected.

"Really? Are you sure, because I thought—"

"Shut *up*!" barked non-Fleming. He patted me down

and found my lighter, comb, and wallet, which he tossed on the floor. When he discovered all the bulges in Norm's vest, he ordered it removed and dropped into a clunking heap. "What are you, fool?" he wondered out loud. "Some sort of human hardware store?"

It was then that I saw Norm had palmed what looked like a silver fountain pen. I knew instantly what the slender, shiny instrument was and shook my head, which caused the pain to lance back. A single-shot tear-gas pen was no match for a revolver.

But the Defender of Justice wasn't built that way. He cocked the defensive weapon with his thumb and began to turn.

I said, "Sonova—" and went low at our assailant's legs, catching some of the exploding gas when Norman fired.

My opponent's gun erupted twice above my head. Each shot wanged something high and echoed off the ceiling.

My eyes began to blur from the dispersed gas, but I could still find the guy with the gun, because he was a screamer. We went down together and he bit into my left forefinger as I tried to squeeze the living shit out of his throat. I grunted like a bull and slammed a shoulder into his side. The gun flew into the darkness between a star and a comet, as the enemy struggled, kicked, broke free, and ran for the exit.

"Stay here, this time," I shouted, lurching to my feet.

"Or get the cops. But do not follow me."

Back out in the warehouse yard, under a moon half obscured by passing clouds, I could hear the footfalls dashing in the direction of the rustling water.

I banged my sore knee rounding the edge of a stack of skids and came to the foot of the tumbling waterfall that slid down a series of wide, rounded rocks. The footing was slick and tricky. The sound of the rushing water was a constant white noise. Shadows cast by the moon in the trees slid back and forth, almost hypnotically. I bent and cupped water in my hand, applying its cooling power to the lump at the base of my head.

A loud splash farther up the falls caught my attention and I sloshed myself to the next mini waterfall only a few yards behind and below the man I was after.

I slipped and got drenched, while he gained distance up another rising tier of limestone. Wiping water from my eyes, I saw a small sandy beach and pool down below us. High above, colored lights dangled, indicating the top of the slithering falls flowing freely three or four hundred feet above our heads.

The guy was scrambling up and getting away.

I grunted and positioned my injured leg in the strong current. We both struggled on and up, climbing to the left side of the torrent where the power of the falling water was weaker.

I almost lost my footing again as a boulder the size of a beach ball bounded past. From a hundred yards below, I heard Norman shout, "Stop! I have your gun and I'll use it!"

The roar of the streaming water snatched away my soggy response. "Don't shoot!"

I heard the man above me call out the exact same words, but I guess Norm didn't.

"Duck, Mr. Wade," he yelled and fired twice up the dark falls.

The revolver's kick threw him back against his wounded leg and flipped him over into a deep pool.

I hissed water from between clinched teeth and started back down, when a body abruptly bounced past me, splashing, and clutching at the wet rocks to my right, before sliding beyond my grasp into another dark pool past where Norm had gone under.

I rode the water over the lip of a smooth stone and came to where Norman floated sideways in a mound of foam. He coughed and flailed around so much that I had to pull him to dry land, or we'd both drown.

"Did I get him?" he spat.

The Noir Man wanted to dunk him again.

CHAPTER 13

The boy's name is Bobby Marley," Whiteside said. "He a fun musician, partyin' at the Fest when he hear da gun go off. Dat's how da police find you and we catch up."

I wrung water out of my pants legs, while Fleming gave a twenty-pound note to an overjoyed Jamaican youth. The kid smiled and clasped the bill before him, backing away and bowing like he was leaving the court of Saint James.

Once again, we'd been questioned by Jamaican officials and, once again, Fleming had covered for us. This time our freedom seemed to have hinged on a handful of British currency.

After spending ten minutes searching the falls and

finally locating Norm's glasses, we collected our possessions from the warehouse.

Moving around in wet clothing was actually a refreshing alternative from the island's oppressive heat.

Whiteside assisted Norm into the back seat of the Sunbeam, but decided to stay at the celebration, promising to again try and locate the imposter for us.

"With luck," Fleming said, putting the car into gear, "the man drowned in the falls of Dunn's River and washed out to sea. The police will likely find the body there."

"That crazy commie almost drowned me," Norman said from the darkness of the back seat.

I turned to glare at his still drenched face. "The next time I tell you to stay put, you stay put."

"What? Am I Lassie or Nit-Nit-Nir?" he complained.

"You got caught and could have been killed. I'm not ready for that, yet."

"So did you."

He had me there, but I persisted. "You almost drowned and I had to stop and save you."

"Well, I saved us both by firing that gun, *thankyouverymuch*."

Damn. Checkmate. But I didn't give him the satisfaction of a response. We both just sat there steaming, figuratively and literally, in the warm night.

"Why does your friend hate the Communists?" Fleming asked.

"He had relatives killed behind the Curtain," I grumbled, taking hold of the wooden cane, just because it felt good to grab something.

"I see," the novelist replied. "That is quite enough for anyone."

There was a pause and we were now driving slowly through the crowded streets, past joyous throngs tumbling out of bars and cafes. This ska music was the Hit Parade of the island.

"We'd best not return to Goldeneye," Fleming advised quietly. "Kaminski still could be out there and he's probably associated me with you by now." The novelist reached out his left arm and fumbled open the glove box in front of me. "Take this," he said, handing me a .25 Beretta, while easily navigating a sharp turn on the A3. "It's a ladies gun, but all I have at the moment."

Fleming pretended not to have knowledge or resources to deal with danger, but when circumstances forced his hand, he was right there, ready to act.

I held the cool little weapon in my damp palm while we accelerated into a night layered with darkness and gathering fog. "Where to, then?" I asked.

"We'll visit Firefly," Fleming mused. "I usually play bridge with Noel Coward there on Tuesday evenings anyway. Who knows?" he arched an eyebrow at me. "He might need a fourth."

"My leg is starting to throb again," Norm announced from behind us. "I could use a fifth."

I turned and stared at my friend.

"You should see the look on your face." He laughed, but it ended with a sneeze.

I sighed and shook my head, feeling the pain at the back of it and hearing water gurgle in my left ear. "You can be the dummy."

"That's a bit harsh, don't you think?" Fleming commented, continuing to concentrate on the road before and behind us. He certainly played things guardedly for a mere author of popular fiction.

With the windows rolled down, and the heat, I was almost dry by the time we arrived.

Firefly was a lot like Goldeneye, only larger, cleaner, and higher up on a cliff overlooking Port Maria Bay. There was another small river down a ravine at the back of the clipped lawn with mauvish rocks and feathery bamboo bushes climbing up the hill.

The estate's owner, a self-presumed knight of the realm, was a jolly-well, balding man with a slight orange complexion, even under his tan. Noel Coward, dressed in tan shorts, a pale green shirt, and a red scarf loosely knotted at the neck, greeted and took us in as if we were old school chums.

"The island still has its magic, don't you think, Ian?" Coward asked as we stepped through the vine-covered entranceway. "But it's losing its charm to the tourist trade. Well, don't stand on ceremony. Come in and join us. I've just fixed a fresh batch of martinis."

I had never been in a place before with so many framed photographs of its owner on display. There were pictures on walls and in stands of Coward in uniform during the war, Coward in Hollywood with Jane Powell, and Coward at Drury Lane with Michael Redgrave. Clearly, this Coward was vain.

He had a baby grand piano stuffed into one corner of the estate's main room, which I should have expected, since I knew he'd composed so many tunes and musical plays through the years. What I didn't expect were the paintings he'd created and scattered about the bungalow. Several were populated by young men and the one on his easel illustrated a well-endowed lad standing nude on a sun-filled beach.

The artist caught me looking at it and came over to lightly place his hand on the back of my shoulder. "I usually paint over the body and add clothing before I exhibit my work in public. You're getting an exclusive show, m'lad."

I got the distingue impression that he was pretending to be Waldo Lydecker in *Laura*, but I kept my eyes fixed on the easel. "Your work strikes me as a little crude," I judged.

He smiled. "Excuse me?"

"Nothing. I didn't say anything," I said and I eased past him to stand near a rat-tan sofa that held a man who was Coward's opposite, Errol Flynn.

"Don't let the old boy get you down, Streak," warned

the once-handsome actor. "And I mean that both ways." He knocked back a half glass of iced vodka. "Flaming middle-age."

While Norm and I changed into dry clothes on loan from our host's surprisingly large wardrobe, Fleming informed Coward and company of our recent unscheduled visit to Cuba. The florid, fifty-year-old Flynn said that he'd spent several days with Fidel Castro earlier in the year while making *Cuban Rebel Girls*.

"I was just in Havana, too," Coward contributed as I came back to join the small crowd. "Playing in a film with Alex Guinness,"

"Yes, that would be the new Carol Reed picture, *Our Man In Havana*," I offered, which got me a lot of stares.

"My dear boy," the playwright said. "You *are* well informed, indeed."

I felt my face redden a bit. "I read the trades," I explained—which was true, but sounded silly here in the middle of the Caribbean.

"The film is all about spies and based on one of Graham Greene's novels," Coward informed through a toothy smile. "I portray a double-agent."

Norm didn't seem to know Coward from Cromwell, so he kept quiet—or else he was near fatigue. I kept a close eye on him.

"I've read the book, of course," Fleming said, as if anyone really cared to listen. "But I prefer Somerset Maugham over Greene any day."

"That I'd like to see," Coward grinned.

It was like watching a British version of Martin and Lewis, only with two Deans.

I interrupted the festivities by asking if we could possibly set up a call back to the States. Coward had to try three circuits and two different operators before we could get Walt on the line.

After all that, Fleming had the embarrassing task of asking our host and Flynn to leave us in private. "The way I figure it," Fleming said, "my imposter brought Wade here to get him off familiar turf to kill him."

It was late afternoon, back in LA as the filmmaker's voice issued from the tiny amp that Norm had jury-rigged to the telephone. "Yes, it's now been confirmed that your man was in the employ of Nickolas Reed."

"He tried to take me out twice before," I said.

Fleming gestured to indicate that I didn't need to shout at the telephone. He added in an even voice, "This time, he must have figured he'd have more luck, if you were out of the country."

"So we should have stayed home all along, huh?" Norm whispered.

Fleming gave him a scowl. "When Kaminski initially adopted my identity in Los Angeles, he might have thought it would be a bonus if he could embarrass or expose me, while killing Wade."

"So, you think he had nothing to do with the skyjacking?" Walt said.

I leaned forward as if a couple of inches made a difference in transcontinental communications. "Once the air-heist drew so much public attention, he feared that his impersonation would be quickly exposed."

"So he faked his heart attack, hoping to get away from us long enough to go poof, huh?" Norm said.

"Any chance that your people can locate him?" Fleming asked the voice on the phone. "Assuming that he's still among the living."

"I'll have someone look into it." The amplifier crackled. "At the moment, I'd expect he'd be trying to make contact with Reed or to get back to Europe, possibly."

That made me wonder. "It must be pretty hard to track anyone from Jamaica to Europe—when you're sitting in LA"

"You'd be surprised, Stan," Walt said. "Current reports say that Reed doesn't what to kill you anymore."

"Oh?" I said. "Nice to know that I'm no longer a target."

"Maybe that's exactly what he wants you to think," Fleming said.

My head was starting to hurt again.

"The game has changed," Walt went on. "They've gotten their hands on an important operative, known as Agent Poole, in Germany."

Now Fleming was the one to lean forward. "Well, that puts the hair in the butter. We need to effect an immediate rescue."

"I agree," Walt's voice quickly came back. "It might be a golden opportunity, Stan, if you joined Fleming on a trip to Heathrow airport, as my intelligence agent."

"England?" Norm asked.

"Besides," Fleming said, looking up. "We need someone who has no previous connection with MI-6."

"Oh, I see," Norm said. "Fresh bait, huh?"

I had an idea to share. "You say that it'd be a golden opportunity, Walt, but it might be even more golden, if you joined us all there, yourself. I'm tired of being a Mickey Mouse pawn." I could almost hear him purse his lips in thought, so I gave an ultimatum. "Get in the game, or I'm out, Walt."

The amp sighed. "All right. I half expected that you'd say something like that. I can have Roy take over for me for a few days here and check up on a couple of productions we have operating near London."

"Fine, but plan to spend the bulk of your time working on this Agent Poole thing," I warned. "Or else I'm on the next flight out of here for Los Angeles."

"Me, too," Norm added. "Remember, I was shot."

"That's right," I went on. "Norman was shot during the skyjacking and *he's* going on."

"I am," Norm nodded. "I am? For real?"

"You can stop trying to sell me on the idea," Walt conceded. "I'll meet you all in England in a few days. I guess I owe you that much, Stan."

Which was all I needed to hear. Any doubts I had

about travelling across the Atlantic were carried away in a Gulf Stream of relief and respect. Even the Noir Man seemed satisfied.

Immediately following the end of the phone call, Fleming said, "I can't believe that you just bluffed the Grey Seal."

"He probably has an ulterior motive," I said.

"Do you really think he'll meet us at Heathrow airport?" Norm asked.

"It will be the first time in a long while that the old boy got back into the game, as you put it," Fleming said,

"Some game," Norm commented. "Our Man from Uncle Walt."

Fleming lit another cigarette and, through the swirls of smoke, said, "Welcome to the cold war."

"But how can the FBI work overseas?" Norm asked. "I thought that was illegal somehow."

"Honestly, it happens far too often," Fleming said. "Your Federal Bureau can investigate on foreign soil when there are suspected attacks on embassies or consulates. We'll simply be following up on established criminal activities. We can inform your CIA later of our findings."

The logic of that sounded weak to me, but the writer went on to promise Norm and me diplomatic passports identifying us as "couriers" of Her Majesty.

It all seemed feasible, doable, if not fully practical. I'd been following Johnny Hazard in the Sunday comics sections and *he* was in London on a case, so why not? Get it done. Except this was no comic.

When the three of us came back into the main room of the house, Noel Coward was already shuffling his bridge cards. "Now then," he smirked, with a glinting eye, "who's ready for a rubber?"

PART III
GOLDENHEART

CHAPTER 14

We touched down in England two days later in the rain. Unlike Jamaica, the London climate was nothing like that of my native LA. Here it was at least thirty degrees colder on anybody's scale and wet with little or no sign of the sun. As Chiefs Thundercloud and Thunderthud used to say, "Ugh 'em."

I had to admit that my leg was better, but Norman's had become slightly infected by his dunking in the falls at Dunn's River. He'd also caught cold and now sneezed more than I did, even with my sinus condition.

During the flight, he'd chewed my ear off about a new *Green Lantern* comic he'd read last week. It was an update, he said, of an old *Green Lantern* comic and the new character would team someday, he thought, with the new Flash to create a new Justice Society, he predicted.

I couldn't keep track of all this, especially since Norm had that nasty "code in his dose." Like Ian, I let my eyes slowly drift shut and hoped I didn't snore, like Ian.

The Jamaican police had not been able to get a line on the Yuri "Fleming." If he was still kicking around, it could be that he caught one of a hundred boats out to one of a dozen islands in the West Indies that sported an airport, and was chortling at us from anywhere in the world.

Thus, I kept looking over my shoulder.

As we de-planed, we were met by a trim red-head, whom Ian introduced as Molly Marie O'Dee. She could have passed for a young Debbie Reynolds, somewhere between *The Daughter of Rosie O'Grady* and *The Affairs of Dobie Gillis*.

"Ha-ware-ya?" she asked, shaking hands all around. "Ian informed me to expect ya. I've a car waitin' outside. Annie baggage?"

I quickly learned that this lass's accent came and went depending on her mood. Sometimes it was so thin you could cut it with your elbow, while other times you'd need a chainsaw. In all cases, I figured it was false, but then again, she did have a face of faint freckles and her eyes held a lilt of green like shamrocks, so...

"There ya go now." She smiled as we climbed into a taxi-motor cab. Directing her attention to Ian, she cooed, "How are ya keepin, sir?"

Fleming briefed her on our situation while we rode into London proper and got a room at a modest hotel on

Commercial Street near Whitechapel Road.

"Jack da Ripper used to oberate around here, huh?" Norm asked.

Both Ian and Molly quickly learned not to respond to most of Norm's comments.

We unpacked and made plans to meet down in the hotel restaurant for dinner.

I filled the time walking around a few blocks outside under a hotel umbrella, a misty downpour, and gray sky. "So, this is London," I said to no one, while sounding like Edward R. Murrow.

The slick streets seemed to be less than one lane wide and the air was filled with the smell of fried fish. In the distance, I saw a darkly cloaked figure and thought of Norm's comment about the Ripper. It turned out to be a Bobby in a macintosh whipped by a gale.

In some strange way, the chill or the fact that I was in an environment different from back home made me suddenly desperate for a smoke. I resisted the urge by counting the cars that sped through the intersection. Five went to the right; three went left; and eleven, plus a single motorcycle, went straight down Commercial Road on what, to me, was still the wrong side of the street. Yeah, different, all right.

I'd planned my casual stroll down the London pavement as a way to see if it would draw any undue attention, and I got my answer.

No one took the slightest interest in Stan Wade, secret agent, which was good and a little sad. I went back into the hotel lobby and wired a dozen red roses to Suzi with a card that said, "Wish I weren't here, sweetheart. Back soon. Standy."

Walt's flight had arrived the day before and he'd been out at Pinewood studios checking on production of his *Kidnapped* movie shooting there. He was already waiting and accompanied by a young blond man at a center table when we entered the small establishment's dining area. The young man was a local actor with a highly suggestive name, Peter O'Toole, who had a small role in the new movie and wore too much Vitalis. We all caught a whiff of V-7 during dinner.

"So you're Walt Disney?" Ian said. "The Grey Seal."

Walt puffed on a fag. "I'm not Disney anymore. Disney is more than one man now."

"Sounds vaguely religious," Fleming commented, sipping a martini.

"A thing, not a who," Walt replied, unshaken.

I made a sound like an owl and the two men grudgingly shook hands. Walt had shaved off his mustache as a sort of disguise and that's when I noticed that Fleming had apparently started growing one for the same purpose. I couldn't help running a finger over my own bare upper lip. A bored, balding waiter patiently, um, waited, while I tried to find something I liked on the menu card.

"You're American?" the slump-shouldered man asked, holding pencil to pad, still waiting.

I gave up on the menu and looked up into his sad eyes. "Yes, what do you recommend?"

Without expression, he said, "Eat all of your vegetables and remember the Alamo."

Norm almost choked into his water glass.

Fleming and I shared a couple of brandy and sodas. He drank the brandy and ordered some sort of roast beef item for me as we all settled in to get to know each other better.

Ian's support person, Molly O'Dee, said her favorite movie was *The Quiet Man*, but that felt too pat. She professed being awe-struck at meeting a genuine American PI, "like on the telly," and kept asking me what happened to Flyface. I had to explain to Ian that Flyface was the villain currently running in *Dick Tracy*.

"Have ya killed anyone, Mr. Wade?" she wanted to know.

"Not since last June nineteenth."

"Seriously, now?"

"I'd rather not go into it."

Fleming said that he thought I was full of Hollywood.

"Sorry," I said. "Whenever I'm stressed, I tend to slip into Bogart mode."

"Aye." Molly nodded. "The USA movie tough guy in *The Big Sleeping Falcon*."

Norm giggled and told Molly that she was charming.

As it turned out, O'Dee wasn't her real name and she

wasn't really Irish. "I took the name from the river Dee in county Cavan," she confessed. "And I'm a wizard with knives and chess, I am."

Norm quickly suggested that they play together—a little too quickly, I thought. The O'Toole guy used his deep blue eyes and soft voice to try and win her interest, but she brushed him off elegantly, seeming to prefer Norm's company. Before the meal ended, the actor had excused himself and gone to the bar. The next time I looked around, he was gone and I never saw him again except on the big screen.

Molly tilted her head toward Walt. "Do tell us again, why they call ya the Grey Seal."

He cleared his throat. "Oh, when I was young, I used to dote on the *Adventures of Jimmy Dale* by Frank Packard. Jimmy went around solving mysteries and fighting crime under the identity of the Grey Seal."

Norm went, "Eh?"

Walt pushed back his chair slightly. "He always left a kind of gray calling card, sort of like the sign of Zorro." He wiggled his index finger and went, "Swish, swish, swish."

I just stared at this performance.

"What?" Walt asked. "You don't think I was ever young?"

"I don't think you ever grew up," Ian said,

Walt pretended to run him through with an invisible sword, saying, "Touché."

Gradually, the conversation turned to our trip to East Berlin to find this Agent Poole. I wondered aloud why I needed to be involved. Ian wondered, too.

"This is not the place to discuss that," Walt said. "Besides, we'll know more when we get there."

'*Walt is playing you again,*' the Noir Man said.

For once, I had to agree and tried to casually probe for more information.

"I'm a relatively clever guy," I said to Fleming, "and you seem clever, too. Would you mind telling me what I've gotten myself into?"

"You can never be sure of things in this world, no matter how clever you think you are," the writer said, waving out a match he'd just used to light a Player's cigarette. "A girl came to me one time, saying her father was going to shoot himself. I ran up to his room and told the old gent that killers were after me. I needed a gun, quick. He gave me his pistol and I left him, thinking how clever I'd been. He'd never know that I'd lied about the killers as a ploy to get the gun away from him. Then I found out that he simply jumped out the window."

"So, no matter how clever you are," I said, "things can still go wrong."

Fleming sighed. "Very easily."

"Oh," Norm said through a stuffy nose, "Can I use dat in da nobvel I'm writing? Id's called, *My Gun is Slow and Steady.*"

Fleming looked at him coolly. "Absolutely not."

"Oh…just asking."

The dinner had been surprisingly tasty and wholesome, but the room seemed thick with spies. I folded my napkin and set it on the table. "Thanks, Ian, I think. Your story made me feel much better. Like I'm trapped in a riddle, wrapped in an enigma, inside a mystery novel." But something in Fleming's story stuck with me for a long time.

We spent the rest of the evening up in Fleming's room, making plans based on the scant information we had from various sources. The writer learned from Molly's contacts in the British Secret Service that Nicholas Reed was rumored to be in East Berlin with the captured Agent Poole. Germany was split in half after WWII and its capital Berlin happened to be in the Eastern portion, itself split into four sectors, with only one, the easternmost, controlled by Russia. Nick Reed's demands from there involved me, probably out of revenge for my part in his brother August's death earlier in the year.

This spy stuff was all upside down and backward to my normal way of operating, back in the good old United States. I guess that's why they call it "foreign intrigue." If Mr. P had taught me anything about investigations, it was to methodically, doggedly stay with the case. But I wondered if that applied to the double-dealing world I was in now. Aside from Norm, everyone else in the room seemed to be hiding something.

I found that I was staring at Norman's friendly face

as if he were one fixed point in a changing universe.

He caught me. "Wad?"

I shifted my gazed to Ian. "So give us the background dope on Nicholas Reed."

"There's not much to tell, really," he admitted. "There are no photos of him. At first, we didn't even know August Reed had a brother."

"Moly hackeral!" Norm said. "Just like *The Man Called X*, huh?"

I glared at him, wondering why again I'd brought him along. Oh, yeah—friendly face.

"Well," he mumbled, blowing his nose into a handkerchief, "at least I didn't say *Great Ganymede*."

Fleming went on. "Nicolas was the youngest of the two brothers, born in Kiev in 1921."

I calculated. "So he's at least thirty-eight. Any distinguishing features? Walks with a limp?"

"Ah…possibly. Accounts vary on that point."

"Affects a knowledge of rare books, but hasn't any?"

"Beg your pardon?"

"Never mind. So he's a man of mystery."

"He is that. But I've got our top people working on it and we'll know more soon."

I switched topics, trying to find firmer ground. "And who, exactly, is this Agent Poole, anyway?"

Molly seemed more interested in this subject than I'd expected. "Aye, I'd like to know more aboot that pairson maself."

Fleming shot Walt a glance to indicate that the ball was in his court.

Walt appeared to have anticipated the question. He snuffed out his cigarette, eased back in his chair, and took a deep breath. "That's—" he said, as I leaned forward, "—classified."

"Wad!?" Norman screeched.

"Come on, Walt," I said, almost upsetting an ashtray with the sweep of my open hand. "That's horseshit and you know it."

Fleming edged between us. "Well, I know that Agent Poole has a long history of successful operations, the most recent being undercover work with another American agent who died during the shooting of that *Ben Hur* movie in Italy."

Walt said nothing, so Fleming went on. "Backchannel chatter has it that the agent who died during filming was secretly involved in high-level Central-European espionage operations. And that his death would be an embarrassment to your nation. The Soviets plan to use Agent Poole in order to capitalize on the matter and its immediate cover-up. It will be a coup for them if Agent Poole gives up the necessary information and confirms the rumor as the truth."

"How do we know we can depend on this guy keeping his mouth shut?" I asked. "What if he's made a secret deal with the Russians and is only pretending to be captured?"

"This is simply a rescue operation," Walt said, firing up another cigarette. The reflected flame gave his face an odd highlight, illuminating it with un-guessed strength. "And you're wrong for two reasons. One, Agent Poole has been a loyal operative for over fifteen years. During that time, several highly financial offers have been made in the past and turned down flat."

"And the other reason?"

"He's a she."

Okay. Play your silly game, I thought. "Isn't that irrelevant?"

Walt puffed quietly. "Not always. And not in this case. The important thing is that the opposition is bound to apply pressure or resort to drugs. It's only a matter of time."

"Which is why we must move quickly," Molly mused, "ta save the poor woman."

No one argued the point as the meeting broke up, but I still had what felt like reasonable doubts.

ↄ๏ↄ

The next morning, Molly called my room. "Ah, yar awyke," she purred and invited me to breakfast. "That white streak in yar hair is very sex-xy."

"I'll be down in ten minutes."

Seated in the near-empty restaurant, after we'd ordered, she confided that she'd conducted a "Wee-bit-o spyin" the evening before and had overheard Ian and Walt talking together last in the night after we'd all retired.

"Can I ask ya a question?"

"Of course," I replied, noting the stirring effects of her lilac perfume. She wore a thin scarlet ribbon around her neck and I just couldn't take my eyes off it.

"Would ja like for me ta give ya a blow—"

"Hold it!" I said, stiffening my neck and one other place.

Her green eyes searched mine, as she continued, "—by blow description of what I heard them discussin'?"

My heart rate slowed to normal. "Just hit the high points."

"Well," she breathed. "They thought you might be a sort of barginin chip with Agent Poole and kept talkin aboot ya two."

"Both me and Norm?"

"I'm not certain exactly. It sounded more like ya two were a kinda codename or somthin'."

I was beginning to feel lost again and it was only nine o'clock in the morning. I realized that I was going to have to adapt to her new information or ignore it. I didn't like the sound of the bargaining chip comment and frankly didn't care much what happened one way or the other to Agent Poole. "I'm not here to play games," I told her. "I'm here for one reason only and that's to get a crack at the people who threatened me and killed Max."

Her smile froze for a second, but she seemed to accept my words as the final comment on the subject, adding, "I love a tough guy."

We finished our poached eggs and bacon and, an hour later, we were back in Ian's room with the other three tough guys. He distributed flight information and altered passports. We each needed a new profession if we planned to go into East Germany, behind the Iron Curtain. Walt was now a film importer from Hollywood. Ian and Molly were travel writers for separate British newspapers. Norm and I were reporters from the *Saturday Evening Post*.

Norm was a little disappointed. He'd had his heart set on getting a "secret identity" and a new name during the mission behind enemy lines. He wanted to play the role of a successful Pasadena businessman and already had a name picked out: Mr. Martin N. Lewis.

"Some other time," Fleming said, handing out German Marks and a few small diamonds to each of us. "These roles will make more sense once we meet our contact in West Berlin."

Walt seemed satisfied, but warned, "The entire city will soon be barracked and blocked, East to West, with barbed wire, high walls, and even land mines. All in order to stop the daily flow of hundreds of refugees to the West."

"Hmm," I mused. "And we'll be going the other way, like lambs to the slaughter."

Fleming smirked. "I can see that you are a man of quick intelligence."

'*Cheeky bastard*,' said the Noir Man.

"'Fret not thyself because o' the ungodly.' Psalm 37, verse 1," Molly said.

There was nothing to say to that.

But Norm advised, "A greab man once said, 'We cannot hab peace widout sacrifice.'"

"Who?" I asked.

"I don't know, but it sounds greab, huh?"

CHAPTER 15

Once we landed at the Tempelhof airport in West Berlin, we pretty much knew what our next move would be. After an uneventful flight, if you didn't count the fact that Norm was airsick again, we filed through customs and gathered at a table near the big window-wall of the airport lounge. Through the plate glass, I could see a bright green BP truck refueling the wing tanks of our DC-6.

Molly had been to West Berlin before and told us how her ex-partner had died here, falling screaming into a band saw, sliced to shreds.

Norm was certain that she'd made up the tale just to confound us, but she swore, "He was an arse, in the end," and chuckled lightly at her own pun. I was never going to understand British humor.

"There's no peace, saith my God, to the wicked," she added with a wink. "Isaiah 57, verse 21."

Not to be fully taken in by her tale, Norm immediately came back with, "Yeah, well, who's the straightest man in the Bible?"

Molly glanced at all of us, hoping for an answer and then shrugged, "I dinno?"

"Joseph, since Pharaoh made da ruler of him. Genesis 41, verse something."

"The only thing older than yesterday's espionage information," Walt commented, "is a bad joke like that one."

I had to agree and I said that it was a sign that the diverse members of our little team were beginning to bond.

This last word caused Fleming to suspect yet another pun, which I didn't understand at first until Norm said through his stuffy nose, "You dough—James Bond?"

A cloud of black smoke puffed out of the starboard inboard engine of the shining DC-6, as the prop began to turn. It felt like my last chance to get out.

'*Quit while you're ahead,*' the Noir Man insisted.

I found myself yearning to be back on my boat, safe and listening to cool jazz. And that reminded me again of the last time I'd seen Max. I owed him to continue on with this affair to its conclusion, wherever that led.

"Anyone know who that guy in the tweed suit is?" I asked. "He's been watching us and is now coming over."

Like Molly, Fleming apparently had been to West

Berlin before. Our approaching contact man turned out to be a German theoretical physics professor named Herbert Franke, who enjoyed drinking beer and smoking cork-tipped cigarettes. Norm was delighted to learn that the solid-looking man with the lazy smile also dabbled in science fiction and had arranged for our happy crew to attend a small conclave of "sci-fi" writers in the Soviet side of the city.

Our reason for going to the East would be based on that literary event. Ian was to pretend to be working on an idea for a sequel to his airplane-car novel, *Chitty-Chitty Bang-Bang*. Walt was thinking of casting Fred MacMurray in the picture. And I was supposedly researching the concept of putting a time-machine in the flying vehicle. All perfectly sane cover stories for science fiction, but Norm said, "Dat's da stupidest thing I eber heard of," and sneezed again.

We piled into a couple of waiting taxis and drove to the Café Marquardt on Kurfurstendamm, not far from the gutted ruin of the Kaiser Wilhelm Memorial Church. The bombed out tower of the church stood on its traffic island as a solitary reminder of the war, silhouetted against the glass facades of new office buildings.

West Berlin didn't strike me as a particularly friendly town. The streets were clogged with those bug Beetle cars, like an infestation.

The tram noises and distant screeching of the U-Bahn as it took a big curve into the zoo station accompanied our light lunch of schnitzel and potatoes with cream.

From there we walked a short block to the Hotel Kempinski, near the Brandenburg Gate. The big and brooding structure was set in a small park, less than a hundred yards from a railway underpass. In the old days, the building might have been a town house, but it had come down in the world since then.

Franke got us checked in and then begged off from any further association with our party. We were on our own, but this smoke and mirrors stuff appeared to be a piece of cake, easy as pie. I hoped the menu wouldn't change.

After a shower, I found that my suitcase had been searched. When we got back from sharing a drink in the hotel bar, it appeared that it had been searched again. Under the circumstances, I could hardly wait to see what would happen when we got to the Soviet sector.

Norm's condition became worse. He was feverish now from his infected leg. I knew that he would have to stay behind here in the West and hoped that Molly could supply him with protection and medical assistance. "You two can play chess and wait for our call," I said.

Molly accepted this mildly, but Norm still insisted on going along.

The Irish lass began combing her auburn hair, trying to entice him. "Yar one hep cat, Norman, ma lad. Stay awhile with me until yar feelin better."

But he still wasn't buying it, saying that he'd be letting me down. "Mock my words, you're gonda need me." Then he gave a harsh, liquid cough.

"Look," I reasoned, "when things get grim, you're the guy I go to for help and to lift my spirits. You're not just my Tonto, Bernardo, or Alfred. You're my partner, buddy. We can't both be down at the same time, right?"

"I guess..." he said in a voice that sounded like Andy Devine's and then he sneezed again.

"Bless you. Okay then," I said, taking a small key from a flap in my wallet. "If I don't make it back, use this on a safety deposit box at the CalFed bank. I want you to have what's inside and—"

"Is dis where the bodies are buried?" he asked, accepting the key.

"—and tell Suzi that I love her."

"She lobs you too. She said so before we left. An' subthing else, but—"

"I've got one for you," I went on. "Have you heard? It's in the stars. Next July we collide with Mars."

He nodded and completed the lyric with: "Well, did jew eber. What a swell party dis is."

"That's absolutely right. Swell party," I said, handing him Karloff's cane. "Now stay off that leg. You can pretend to be Bat Masterson with that walking stick. Get me?"

"Gotcha good," he replied, sniffling.

"Look after him, Molly," I said. "Get him to tell you

all about Jack Kirby, the Green Ashcan, or Phil Dick. We should be back by then."

As I closed the door behind me, I heard her ask him about Flyface. They'd get along just fine together.

ⴻⴰⴰⴰ

Walt and Ian were arguing. They did that a lot.

"You make films, for God's sake," Fleming protested. "What do you know of real life?"

"Stagecraft is much like spycraft," Walt replied, waving his lit cigarette. "Remember how we held you all together during the war?"

"The war?" Fleming bristled under his growing mustache. "Why you insufferable—"

"Hey!" I shouted. "Do I have to separate you two? Keep it together until after Operation Bay City."

"What's that?" they both asked, which was my intent all along.

"What we're doing now. Named it after the most corrupt city I ever heard of. Seems fitting, don't you think?"

"Well, he's creative," Ian said to Walt. "I'll grant you that." Then he turned to me. "Why are you always joking things up?"

"I don't know," I said. "Probably something I heard about Hemingway. He said a real man performs with grace under pressure."

"Well, we've certainly got the pressure," he allowed. "But we're not going anywhere near the state of Grace."

I tasted bile. Despite what we'd been through together, neither one of these men would let their guard fully down and take me into their confidence. I was beginning to better understand how Norman must have felt at times while learning "eye-craft" from me.

I noticed that the bags under Walt's eyes were almost as large as Bob Mitchum's. His shoulders and back were carried stiffly, as if he'd left the coat hanger in his suit jacket. Coming all the way from LA, he must have been suffering from severe jet lag.

I informed them of my decision to hold Norm back and asked Ian if Molly could protect him while we were gone. He thought it through and agreed that it could be useful to have them waiting at the British station here in the West.

An hour later, we went down to the street and caught a jam-packed city subway into East Berlin. Most of the people in the train were heavily shawled women who had probably taken the risk of crossing over to the West to shop.

The doors closed and the train slid into its dark tunnel. I'd never ridden underground before and found it less unnerving than traveling high above it.

When we stepped off at the Spittelmarkt station in the Soviet sector, we lined up before military guards who searched us for weapons. Ian was pinch-searched and his

Walther 7.65 was confiscated. A serious-faced youth in an ill-fitting uniform only patted me down and I got through with my Beretta still resting in an inside coat pocket. They let Walt keep his Mickey Mouse watch.

As we left the checkpoint, we passed a huge poster showing two Germans in the uniforms of the *Volks Polizei* and the State Security Police. Ian had previously briefed us on the dangers of encountering the Vopos or the MVD. At least the cops of Bay City weren't armed with machineguns like the police here were. *Truth is indeed stranger than fiction*, I thought.

Monolithic blocks of apartment buildings stood guard along the arbitrary line that divided East from West—their doors and windows boarded or cemented, their roofs spotted with small nests of baby machine guns.

In square area, the old imperial capital of Germany was almost as big as Los Angeles. In a few places, there's no high or solid wall across the border, just rows of barbed wire and patrolling military men with occasional guard dogs. There's a no man's land that must have been mined and re-mined, perhaps by both sides. If you set foot there, you'd be blown to bits and bratwurst.

Seeing all the guard towers and fast patrol boats even on the canals that flowed through the city, I wondered how and if we'd ever get back.

But the Rover Boys didn't seem concerned as much as I was. They were back to arguing with each other.

"I hear that your *Sleeping Beauty* was a financial loss," Ian said.

"Let's not discuss it," Walt answered, looking strange without his mustache.

"If I were you," Ian went on, sliding a cigarette into the metal tip of his holder, "I'd be thinking of abandoning animated features. Maybe consider an adult picture? Possibly a Bond movie?"

"Your over-sexed spy-boy doesn't fit my audience demographic."

Fleming shrugged. "Kids grow up before you know it, Walt."

They were so alike and yet so different.

We skipped the science-fiction meeting, of course, and finally spotted our contact man with the red carnation seated alone at a sidewalk table in front of a café. He was a dapper, but plump soul toying with a butter knife and digging at table cloth in what appeared to be bored distraction. Before we could approach him, two Vopos stopped in front of him and escorted him to a waiting car that carried him away.

I caught Walt looking behind us, as if he were searching for someone or something.

"Now what?" I asked.

Ian gestured and we assumed the empty table as the service and table cloth were cleared away for the next customer. *Life goes on in East Berlin, just as it does in the rest of the world. Right?*

While the waiter's back was turned, Ian snagged a salt shaker from another table and shook white powder onto the bare table top, revealing an address that had been carved there. Then he blew the salt away and we left without ordering.

This clandestine spy stuff could be a hoot, if it weren't so dangerous.

We secured rooms that evening at the Lenin hotel, a six-story, wedding cake slab of glass and concrete on the north side of Unter den Linden. We followed the address from the salted table and found it to be what Ian called a "night-fight" club. The entrance to of the Fledermaus Grotto was shabby and un-swept, just as I would have expected of Bay City.

Behind its battered and paint-peeling door, a crowd of at least twenty-five people drank dark bier and shouted encouragement at two bare-knuckle fighters who were going at it inside a ten-by-ten foot roped area in the center of the main room. The collective German voices were so loud it was almost impossible to talk.

One of the fighters was a sumo-sized guy like the Japs I'd once seen tussle together at the Olympic arena. This sloppy, slow-mover, with rolls of body fat and Teutonic folds of flesh at the back of his neck, threw looping punches in slow-mo. His opponent was five-eight or so and much quicker.

As we watched the mismatch, it was obvious that the smaller man scored the majority of points, no matter how this sort of entertainment was measured. The smaller guy was using his speed to avoid the giant, peppering him with rapid sets of deft punches to the big man's forehead and neck. There was already a nasty cut over Sumo's left eye.

Then, through an umbrella of smoke and noise from the crowd, the fat man made an unexpected charge, grabbing the little guy's legs and slamming both of their bodies to the mat.

In the back of the room, at the end of the long wooden bar and under a coat of arms that looked like it had come from a page of Prince Valiant, stood our own opponent, Yuri Kaminski. Walt saw him too, and nudged me before I could shout anything above the screaming audience.

Kaminski did not appear to have noticed us. His head was bent down and forward, his attention centered on a dark-haired, middle-aged woman in a trim, blue dress and too much eye makeup, who threw her head back laughing.

"My god," Fleming said over the din. "He looks nothing at *all* like me. Sharp bony nose. Grizzled hair and high cheekbones. Dark, penetrating eyes that do not flicker."

In the ring, Little Guy landed one effective punch after another into the tub of lard. Both fighters looked exhausted as a bell rang out to end the event. The crowd surged and swayed, elbows flying, while the three of us pushed past the ring and into the back of the hall, moving in on our fake Fleming.

Ring attendants were wiping Sumo's blood off the mat as Yuri made a quick turn, dashing through a door at the back of the bar.

We followed Yuri through the doorway where he'd taken the woman in the blue dress. There were bathrooms to one side and an entrance to the kitchen on the other, but down a long corridor was another door just closing.

I looked at Ian, who nodded. Walt was already moving down the hallway and through the door. We rushed down a rickety flight of wooden stairs and stopped short in a small storage area dominated by a low ceiling and a guy with a gun. The gun was a Luger and the guy was Yuri. "Up with your hands," he ordered, moving the weapon away from me to waver between Walt and Ian.

I tried to use one of those kenpo moves that Suzi had taught me and got it all wrong in the cramped crowded space. My head was still tender from where Yuri had struck it back in Jamaica, and someone with no imagination hit me again now from behind. I went down like a first act curtain. Ian and Walt helped me to my feet. I turned to see that my attacker was the middle-aged woman in the blue dress.

The Noir Man said, '*I tried to warn you,*' as the woman's dark eyes tightened. She took a single step in my direction and slapped my face with a crack that made me see blood red constellations.

Ian and Walt held tightly to each of my arms, keeping me from fighting forward in blind rage. I studied the woman's face and slowly it grew more and more familiar.

And that's how I met Nikkita Reed.

CHAPTER 16

Another she's a he?" I asked Walt.

He looked as surprised as I was. "News to me."

I should have seen it coming, but first I'd been told that the combined US/UK espionage forces weren't aware that August Reed had a brother, right? Then I'd learned that they didn't know for sure where this person was, right? Now, I learned that the brother was really a sister and that Nicolas Reed was actually Nikkita Reed, grand-daughter of John Reed, the turn of the century American reporter and Communist sympathizer. All of this had been wrong, right?

I was royally pissed by this discovery, because, as far as I could see, grand espionage intel hadn't been based on anything certain. It was all just blind guesswork and dumb luck.

One thing for certain, this woman had to be the person who killed Max and tried to kill me.

'*Find a way to kill her, back,*' the Noir Man said.

I struggled to control my hate, as we all raised our hands above our heads in the dank room.

Ian attempted to act like he knew what was going on. "The great Nikkita Reed at last," he said.

I tried to draw her attention. "Nikkita? She's the commie bigwig we've been after?"

She had high, wide cheek bones, almost Asiatic, and a strong jaw that balanced her smirking features. "Take away the letter 'K' from my first name," she said in a silky voice, "and it spells that of our beloved Premier Khrushchev."

Yuri said, "The exposure of your country's spying efforts while making *Ben Hur* is only our minor goal. When presented to the world, it will be another example of the trashy efforts of the West to control the people's minds."

Nikkita agreed, "With Sputnik and the symmetry of Communism, it will be clear that the Communists are winning the Cold War."

"Where is Agent Poole?" Walt asked.

"We have your old woman carefully secluded," she said, "at the rehearsal annex of the Opera House."

I noticed for the first time under her dark eye makeup the sickle-shaped scar that started under her right cheekbone, circled the orbit, and disappeared into the eyebrow. All it needed was a hammer, but that would have pierced her eye.

"We now know that Poole has details of your county's secret high-altitude U-2 flyovers into Russia."

"The game changes again," Fleming said, looking at Walt. "It was only a matter of time before they found out about your spyplanes photographing behind their borders."

I think my jaw must have hit my chin.

"Yes," The film-maker sighed. "But they have no proof."

"Proof?" I said, almost gasping. "Is that why you're really here, Walt? To stop the Soviets from getting proof of our illegal aerial surveillance? Is that the 'ya two' that Molly heard you discussing last night? Did you plan for us to get captured, too?"

Nikkita answered for him. "We'll go public about the flights when we have details of the listening post in Germany that receives signals and processes film. And I assure you, we *will* get those vital details from your Agent Poole. Especially now, since we have you hostage."

"The Cold War will now have peace," Yuri proclaimed. "Peace the way *we* like it."

"You've been reading too many of your own posters," I said. "That's no way to ensure peace."

"Peace through intimidation and strength," Yuri predicted, as the woman began to search us for weapons.

This time, the Beretta was discovered and taken away.

I watched through hate-filled eyes, while Nikkita reached down and caught the hem of her skirt, raising it to access her lower left leg. She tapped the back of her calf and opened a compartment there.

I felt my jaw drop again.

"I always carry trade-tools," she said. "Another reason why we'll win."

"That's ingenious," Ian said.

"In every game, there is always a hidden gambit." She shoved my small gun into a hinged drawer of flesh-colored plastic.

"You're a cripple," Walt taunted.

Yuri laughed, still training the Luger on us.

The dark-eyed woman tilted her head up and gave us a gloating smile. "Border guards never bother with a woman or a prosthetic limb. They never suspect." She lifted a pair of handcuffs from a shelf in the wall next to a rusted electrical box.

"I may want to use that in my next thriller," Fleming said, hands still elevated. "Except villains are always rabidly insane and die near the last chapter."

"Not this time," Nikkita said, going behind us.

"You planned this all along," I said.

"Lured us here with that fake contact man at the café," Walt added.

She didn't answer. Instead, she pulled Fleming's

hands down behind his back and snapped on the cuffs.

From the corner of my eye, I could see her reach for two more pairs of handcuffs. We were under a gun collectively and about to be handcuffed individually.

"This is such a cockup," the writer said. "Tell me this isn't happening."

Without hesitation, she struck him a blow at the base of his skull and he folded up like a wet tent.

"What are you doing?" Walt's voice was almost as high as Mickey's.

"Why not kill them now?" Yuri said.

"We must first attend the meeting with the Head of the HVA and MVD to report on our success and Project Goldenherz."

"Tell them nothing," Yuri spat. "Your ambition will ruin everything."

"Herr Mielke and General Serov can wait," Nikkita ordered through clinched teeth.

"Which one of you Einstein's is in command here anyway?" I asked, trying to get under their skin.

Neither of them showed signs of itching.

"These three will wait for us here—" the woman said and Yuri remained silent as she finished with, "—and sleep."

Fear grew within me.

I had seen guys knocked unconscious a thousand times in the movies, but I knew that in real life, you could be slammed in the brainpan once too often and go into a coma. One more slug, thud, or pounding might cause me to lose my memories, if not my life. If I knew any top secrets, I felt that I'd have given them up right then.

Walt looked at me sternly and saw that, in a small way, I'd been broken, or was about to be. "I've got one for you," he said.

I swallowed. "W—what?"

Nikkita paused. She must have thought he was going to tell her something important.

But instead, he began to sing in an off-key voice: "The way you wear your hat. The way you sip your tea. The memory of all that…" Amazingly, he was doing the lyric game that he'd seen Norm and I play.

My mouth was still dry, but I responded, "No, no. They can't take that away from me."

He nodded with a slight smile. "Grace under pressure."

Clearly frustrated, Nikkita snapped the cuffs shut behind him and struck him solidly in the head. He dropped to his knees and fell quietly on his side.

Then she came for me.

I stared into the dark muzzle of Yuri's gun. She yanked my arms into place, just as she had done with Ian and Walt. I held my fear under control, knowing and dreading what came next. There was a small knife blade taped to the back of my brother's wristwatch, but it would be of no use against the cold steel cuffs that clamped tightly onto my wrists.

"This is partial payment for my brother's death," she breathed into my ear. "Izvineetye."

I was pounded into oblivion.

CHAPTER 17

Someone was singing, "The moon belongs to everyone. The best things in life are free, free, free." The voice was a little flat and in the wrong key.

My serenader was the black-and-white clown. I didn't know he could talk, let alone sing.

"Zippity do-da. They can't take that away from me, bibbity bobbity boo, boo, boo." He toddled over to where I lay surrounded by bunnies, squirrels, and a baby deer. They all seemed to want me to go somewhere.

I twisted up into a sitting position and looked around through blurred eyes like that mole character in *The Wind and the Willows*.

But I wasn't free, free. I was still handcuffed and underground. The little animals had scampered away, replaced by the slumped and inert bodies of Walt and Ian.

We were still in the restaurant's windowless vault. The door at the top of the stairs was shut. The room was otherwise empty and the future bleak.

Trapped and trussed up in the basement of the Fledermaus—a sort of German batcave. I chuckled at the thought, which made my head hurt. Also my shoulder from an old injury and my leg from a new one. Pretty soon, I'd be drooling.

Walt came back to consciousness a few seconds later, slowly sat up, and quickly threw up. These two guys were older than me and not used to a lot of physical punishment. Somewhere along the line, pain had become my familiar friend and that worried me.

"Hey, you all right?" I asked, trying to pull and squeeze my wrists free from the cuffs behind my back. Nothing doing.

I shifted my weight and got up on my knees.

Walt reached for his head and must have realized that his own set of bracelets confined him firmly like a hog-tied calf. "Where am I?" he asked stupidly.

"You're in the happiest place on earth, or under it," I said, tasting something like sarcasm. "Damn. I must have bitten my lip when I fell."

"Too bad it wasn't your tongue," Walt grumbled.

And that's how I knew he was coherent and okay.

Fleming's condition was another matter, however. We called to him, but he didn't answer. I tried to get around to where he lay, so I could check his pulse. I fumbled my fat fingers behind my back and pushed down on the side of his neck. I thought I felt a heartbeat, but couldn't be sure.

"We have to get out of here," Walt suggested.

'*No shit, Sherlock,*' the Noir Man said.

I began to wonder if I was ever going to see the real Walt. "What was that talk about U-2 flights over the USSR? Is that the real reason we came all this way? Did you plan to have us captured so we could draw out those commies?"

"Don't be ridiculous," Walt answered. "Yes, the high-altitude flights are real, have been for some time. But I didn't plan for us to get caught." He adjusted his shoulders. "We're here to keep the East hand from knowing what the West hand is doing."

'*Don't trust him,*' the Noir Man said.

But despite my growing suspicions of his duplicity and my own confusion, I felt we were on the verge of something even more important. It was like when I read a murder mystery and had a flash of inspiration of a plot twist, but still didn't know what it meant.

"Buried alive," Walt said.

I scanned around for something, anything that would address our immediate need to get out of here.

The room was like a crude fall-out shelter—probably had been during the war—dug out of the dark and crumbling German soil, but empty now. No tables, chairs, or other furniture. A single, bare electric bulb hung a few feet above our heads, connected to a power box fixed to wall studs across from the entrance we'd used minutes— hours?—before to enter this hell hole.

The floor was uneven rough cement poured over ancient bricks that lay exposed in the corners of the room. The ceiling was stout wooden boards shored up by posts and crossbeams made into empty shelving.

Ian went, "Uh…" and began to move his legs. Walt went over to study him.

I had been fooled once before by a false Fleming. Could it happen again? Either one or both of these men could still be some sort of double agent or traitor to their country.

'*Get out while you've still got your skin*,' the Noir Man commanded.

Ian moaned again.

I gingerly went up the old wooden stairs, that must have been built when God was two, and tried the door. It gave a little and I thought I could do a dance and kick it open, but then where would we be? We had to get these cuffs off first, somehow.

I went back down the steps and said to Walt, "Shouldn't one of you two have a ring that contains poison or some other spy stuff we could use to get out of here? Like a knife in the heel of your dress shoe?"

Walt cocked his head and gave me a half smile. "Actually, my fountain pen *does* double as a tiny flashlight," he offered.

"Oh, that'll help a lot—once the sun goes down."

Fleming said something I didn't catch.

"He's coming around," Walt announced. "We're a tad older than you, Stan."

"And more experienced in all this, I hope."

Ian sat up. "My wife is thinking of leaving me," he mumbled.

I looked at Walt's somber, questioning eyes. "Oh, which reminds me. Thanks for the new car. Very thoughtful of you."

I saw that I'd stunned and worried him. I felt good about that.

His straight, sandy brows arched. "We have *got* to get out of here," he insisted, "before we *all* go nuts."

"Or worse," I countered. "I've got two of the most creative and secretive guys in the world here with me. Let's come up with something. Now."

"Can one of you chaps get inside my coat pocket?" Ian asked. "I need my cigarette holder."

"Take it easy, old chap," I replied. "You're still loopy."

"I hope we don't run out of air," Walt said, focusing his attention on the door. "Those bastards."

"No," Ian answered. "I think I can unlock these restraints with a broken section of the metal tubing in my holder. Saw it done once during the war."

"You're kidding," I said, coming over to where he sat.

"If we can work it into the keyhole, we should be able to jiggle and release the locking mechanism."

"You *are* kidding, right?" Walt asked.

"Planned to use it in one of my novels," the writer grunted. "But I never had the right circumstances. Until now." He came to his feet. "What is that awful smell?"

"Never mind," Walt said. "Show us."

I turned to Ian and began groping about in the pockets of his coat. My trussed up hands and wriggling fingers found a hard, thin object. "This it?"

"If it isn't," Walt said, "then you're doing something obscene. Let me see what you've grabbed."

I could feel the holder with its tapered plastic on one end and a circular cylinder on the other.

"Try to break it so the metal tip comes to a point," Fleming instructed.

I grasped the thing between my half-numb hands and snapped it in two. The metal part fell to the floor.

"I'll get it," Walt said, kneeling and bending back into a sitting position again.

Ian went down too and turned his back to us. "Now work the sharp flange into the hole of my manacles."

I directed the operation as best I could while the two men slouched together back to back. Maybe they really knew what they were doing, after all.

We spent an eternity like that.

"Ian, move your arms more to the left, your left," I ordered. "Walt, push down more and get your fingers

closer to his right hand. No, the other way. Steady now."
I caught a glimpse of the metal tip sliding into the access
hole. "Now twist your wrist, Walt. Easy. Try it again the
other way."

Ian held his breath. Walt swore. "I'm getting a
cramp."

"Try it again," Fleming growled. "I know it will
work."

They were so close to each other now that I could no
longer see their actions.

"I hope your right hand knows what my left hand is
doing," Ian joshed.

They continued to fumble while I felt an intense urge
for a cigarette, a shot of Scotch, or a way to wipe the
sweat from my forehead.

"I think I've got it," Walt announced.

I looked around the room again for some way to
help, but found nothing. "Come on, guys. You can do it.
You have to before the Reds get back."

Something between them went *click* and Fleming
yanked his arms up over his head, the open handcuffs
dangling from his right wrist.

It took another couple of minutes to get Walt's hands
free and then mine. We were as happy as three Houdini's,
but still needed to figure a way out of our dingy prison.

"If we break down the door," Walt said, rubbing his
wrists and cracking his knuckles, "someone will hear and
see us."

"Not if we create a distraction," Ian countered.

Walt shook his head and winced. "If we create a distraction, they'll just come for us, anyway."

I eyed the electrical box on the wall. "Not if they can't find us."

Behind my back, one of my artful companions inquired, "What are you thinking?"

I turned my head to ask Walt, "Does that pen light you mentioned really work?"

"Of course," he answered, taking a thick fountain pen from the inside breast pocket of his suit coat. "But what good will it do?"

Ian began to catch on. "We need a way to short out the power."

I popped open the switch box. There were no switches inside, just a tangle of pre-war wires and two short rows of electrical terminals.

"If we yank out the wires, we might kill the lights upstairs," Ian went on, "but it might do the same to—"

I cut him off in mid-thought. "We can use the cuffs to bridge the gap between the terminals."

"Once the lights are out," Walt said, clearing his throat, "my flashlight will help us find the way out."

"Still could get electrocuted," Ian said.

I let my fingers do the walking along the loops of my trousers. "I think I can insulate the cuffs with this," I said, pulling my belt free and wrapping its length around my right hand. I slide the belt's tongue through the closed clasp of my handcuffs. "The metal buckle will short out the power and the stiff leather should give me some— protection."

"I don't like the sound of that," Walt advised.

"What other choice have we?"

Nobody answered.

I sighed and turned back to the open power box with its menacing collection of Strickfadden-like circuits. I draped my coat over my head to shield against fireworks and whispered, "Get it done."

Ian went up the stairs to prepare to kick in the door.

Walt switched on the tiny light in his fountain pen.

I clenched my teeth. "Count of three." That wasn't all I clenched.

We exchanged glances and nodded, like we're re- hearsed this a million times.

"One." I tightened my grip on the leather strap. "Two."

"Good luck," Ian hissed.

"The Three Caballeros," Walt said.

'*More like Stooges,*' the Noir Man crabbed.

"Three."

ぐうじ

My hand went up and out. The cuff clanked into place. I heard a sizzle that I hoped wasn't my fist. An in- tense, reddish light flashed through my closed eyelids.

There was a loud pop and a sudden blackness that I hoped wasn't my death. Instead, I was knocked back on my ass as a thunderous crash came from where Ian had stood. I came up in one piece, as if energized by a bolt of lightning. Shazam!

"Door's open," Fleming shouted. "Come on."

We clambered up the stairs, following the thin beam from Walt's flashlight, and scurried down the hallway like rats.

I wasn't sure which one of us said, "Not bad for a broken-down cartoonist, an old scribbler, and a beat-up detective."

I didn't think it was me, but—

"Hurry," Ian called. "Someone will be coming to find out what the hell just happened."

"I thought this was supposed to be a distraction," I panted, "not an attraction."

"We need to think these things through better next time," Walt counseled.

Next time?

We navigated down the corridor and made a left into the club's kitchen. The room was dark and thankfully empty of inhabitants. I almost tripped over a clutter of mops and pails.

"Must be later than we thought," Walt said, casting his beam past a grease-caked grill to what looked like a back exit.

"We must have been out for hours," I deduced,

grasping a door knob and turning it. It wouldn't open.

Fleming flipped a latch above the knob and we spilled out into the East Berlin night.

The buckle on my belt had been warped by the electrical surge and I was having trouble keeping my pants up as we waded through the waist-high weeds and stacks of rubble that stretched away to a deserted cross-street lit by a central cluster of yellowish arc lamps. Far in the distance, I could make out the glittering ribbon of the Zimmerstrasse River on the border with West Berlin, but naturally we went the other way.

It must have been long past the designated curfew hour, for we dodged several light-armored vehicles patrolling the streets, accompanied by motorcycle escorts.

Keeping to the shadows and hugging the walls, it felt like something out of a cloak-and-dagger B-movie. We avoided the big new ten-story block edifice of the Haus der Ministerien, which Ian said was the chief brain-center of East Berlin. At the front entrance of the building, guards were stationed, standing casually in large caps and long coats, but with serious Kalashnikov sub-machine guns slung over their shoulders. I put the collar of my coat up to ward off the night's chill and possible recognition. It didn't help much, but felt satisfying, nonetheless.

My stomach growled. We continued down an ill-lit side street. Walt stumbled on the cracked and buckled sidewalk, almost calling out in surprise, but I dashed around a ruined wall and got a hand over his mouth. He nodded his thanks and nearly fell into a pit that had once been someone's cellar.

Ian seemed to know where he was going. We came back onto the Unter den Linden and passed a statue of Frederick the Great, glistening on horseback in the night. "The State Opera House is just ahead," he whispered, peering around the side of a dark building. "The annex must be in back."

"Makes sense," Walt said. "That's where I'd put it."

Yeah, these spy guys were brilliant thinkers, all right. I couldn't believe that I was following their lead, but they'd pushed me to the point where I was making bad decisions. As if I had any real choice in the matter.

Off we went again into the frustrating night.

CHAPTER 18

The air was crisp with October. The full Jamaican moon had waned to three-quarter. I hobbled along behind my fellow escapees, holding up my sagging pants by hand, since the buckle of my belt had been warped by excessive voltage.

In the distance somewhere, a clock tower tolled a single stroke. I looked at my watch and saw that it was slightly after one a.m.

Following these two men through the dark streets of East Berlin troubled me no end. Why were they involved in all of this? Why were they even here? Ostensibly, they were fighting for Queen and Country and the American Way, but that couldn't be the whole truth and nothing but.

I began to think for the first time about the bigger

picture and the future, rather than my own situation and past. Thirty years from now, I'd be their age. What would the world be like then in, say 1990 or beyond? Would we still be in a stalemate with the Russians? Or would Communism have become the dominant political force on the planet?

Already, England felt to me like a country past its prime. Would America become similarly obsolete and inconsequential? Democracy a thing of the past? Or would the world end in the holocaust of nuclear war? Bombed back to the Stone Age?

And where would I be in the far future? My detective work seemed trivial when compared to the imagined alternatives. All the hype and media blitz from Hollywood wouldn't matter one bit. I'd have wasted my life gumshoeing blackmailers and doing my little justice thing, when the important game had been to stop the Soviets.

As uncomfortable as I was not knowing what these two men were up to, underneath all the secretiveness, it seemed that what they were doing would ultimately matter a whole lot more than my little hill of beans.

I remembered my brother, Josh, who'd died fighting the Japs at Midway. His death mattered a lot to me, but I'd always thought that it wasn't very important to the rest of the world. Maybe I'd been wrong about that. Maybe the small event of his death had a much larger consequence. We might have lost at Midway if Josh hadn't died there, and that loss would have probably changed the course of the war and the world, or at least America's part in it.

I thought again of my parents. Had they too died for their country? Walt had suggested that they'd helped stop the Reds from getting the A-bomb, back in the 'forties. What if, instead, they had held back, unsure of what to do, choosing to stand down at the wrong moment and thus letting the Commies advance too far, too soon?

So, now, what was I doing? Was I going to step aside when needed? Or step up to the challenge, even though I didn't have all the answers, even though I didn't fully get what the hell was going on or where the night led?

Norman hated Commies—with good reason. My parents had apparently died fighting them. My brother had done his duty and given his life for American freedom. And then there was poor Max.

None of them had a guarantee that what they did would pay off in the long run, but they all must have felt it was the right thing to do at the time. To do your duty, even if you don't know that it will ever matter or make a difference. Anything else would seem pointless and selfish.

I had always considered my duty was something simple, like helping other people. Their troubles were my business. And right now, that troubling business came down to trusting Walt and Fleming, even if I didn't know how it would turn out. Blind faith?

For all I knew, rescuing Agent Poole might eventually have major results in the Cold War thirty years from now. And I had to admit that it did, in fact, feel like the right thing to do. Even if it meant my—

"There," Ian hissed, pointing into the heart of darkness. "That's where we're going."

The Berlin State Opera building was four-stories high with a colonnaded front like a Corinthian temple and dark at this hour. Stone stairs flared out from either side and three statues stood regally above the entrance. Surely, stately structures like this were part of the inspiration for our ornate movie palaces back home, halfway in time between the Greeks and Graumans.

The annex was much more modest and modern, only three stories and of plain, square architecture, but yet another armed guard stood out front of the building's closed entrance door. I circled around to the back, hoping to find another way in. A cat in a shadowy alley started my heart racing. Or maybe it was a big rat. What would Marlowe do?

'*Get the hell out of Dodge*,' the Noir Man answered.

I hunched up my trousers and groped on.

Of course, there *was* no back entrance. Not even a window. They had all been bricked up years ago.

I crept back around to a secluded side street in the front where Walt and Ian were quietly arguing about something, again.

"You need to let your characters grow up and have fun," Fleming whispered.

"No chance of that happening," Walt replied. "I caught hell from the public when my characters got drunk in *Davy Crockett*."

"Well, my stories are basically just like yours."

"Ha," I said, coming up to them. "With a little sex in it."

Walt gestured with his chin. "There's a window up on the second floor. Looks like it might be open."

I peered through the night and saw that he was right, maybe. But I couldn't see any way to reach the ledge or roof, except for a string of power lines that stretched about five feet from the back of the Opera House.

"It might be possible to climb up the side of the adjacent building to where those cables cross," I said, immediately regretting the statement.

"You mean go up there like Harold Lloyd?" Walt asked.

I ran my tongue over the cut where I'd bitten my lip earlier and kept my mouth shut.

"If you go in through the window," Ian advised, "you should be able to come out through the front and take the guard from behind."

I tasted blood again, but finally said, "Are you volunteering me for a commando raid?"

"I'm only outlining a potential plan of attack," Fleming whispered. "It's up to you."

Walt surprised me by saying in a low tone, "Forget it. Those power cables probably carry over 400 volts.

He'd have to slide down them to reach the window ledge."

"Dangerous work, that," Ian agreed. "Young man's game, too. Not good for us old folk, but I'll flip you for it."

"Okay," Walt answered. "Have you got a quarter?"

"I've something like one right here," Fleming breathed, tossing and catching a coin in his palm. "What is it?"

"Heads," Walt called.

"No, it's a shilling. You lose."

If there had been crickets nearby, we would have heard them rubbing their little German legs together.

"Look you guys," I reluctantly said. "There doesn't seem to be any other way in and we don't even know for sure that your Agent Poole is still being held in there."

"If she's not," Walt said, "we're all in for a long cold war."

I put my full weight on my sore leg to test its strength. No pain. But I dare not touch the back of my skull for fear that it might fall off. "I know I need my head examined," I mumbled, "but I think I can use my belt again to slide across those cables."

"Ah," Fleming said. "A fascinating and new sort of action hero. Beltman."

I grimaced. "And here I thought we left Norman and his gags back in West Berlin."

Moving slowly and carefully down the dimly-lit

street, I crossed over far from the guard's point of view. I stood there and took in a few lungfuls. Then, I eased myself into a shadowed alcove in the side of the Opera House and clutched at the horizontal seams in the building's façade, pulling myself up a couple of feet at a time.

A car passed slowly on the street below me. I froze. If the driver had glanced over at the right moment, he might have seen my shoes wedged into a crack about six feet above the roadway.

The building's stone surface was gritty with soot and other crud I didn't want to think about.

When I started back up, a sleeping pigeon suddenly awoke and fluttered past my head. My fingers began to ache along with all the other pains I'd collected recently. The light here was worse than down at street level. I had to feel my way up the last six feet, around an overhang, gripping a gutter downspout that wobbled when I transferred my weight across it. Seconds later, I was a true second-story man, still having second thoughts about the whole thing.

I reached around the crumbling, rough corner of the building where the power lines stretched down and across what appeared to be a mile-long chasm to the annex. Flexing my sweaty fingers, I began tugging my trusty belt from the loops of my pants. Why hadn't I thought to use Walt or Ian's belt instead?

'*Because, you're an idiot,*' said my dark passenger.

"Nobody asked you," I countered, deep in my throat.

'*Maybe they should have.*'

"And maybe the sun will come up in the west!"

'*Stop arguing and get going!*'

Doctor Heckle and Mister Jib.

I fastened the top button of my pants into a button-hole of my shirt. It seemed to hold well. Confident now that I was an intercontinental op, I looped the belt over the cable and tested the assembly with a few short tugs.

'*This isn't going to work.*'

"Yes, it is."

The cable sagged as I lowered myself onto its limber expanse. I cast free and resisted the demanding urge to grab the power line with both hands, instead of sliding down the cable via the leather strap.

The belt creaked and sank from my weight, but held. My suspended body began to turn slowly, which I didn't like since it would cause me to face the wrong way and I wouldn't be able to see where to put my feet when I arrived at the annex building's window ledge. Assuming that I ever did.

Gravity slid me most of the way across the gap, but not all the way. I dangled like Dilly Dally a good fifteen feet above the alley. My palms began to put out an enormous amount of sweat, my forehead, too. My shoulder felt like it was being worked on professionally by Gorgeous George.

I stifled a grunt and jerked my body, trying to get the belt moving again.

A faint breeze kissed the side of my face and I thought of Suzi.

I looked down, trying to spot where Ian and Walt waited. Why had I let them talk me into this? Who the hell cared about Agent Poole?

My grip began to weaken. This wasn't a cliff, but I was certainly hanging.

Just like at the end of a serial chapter when I was a kid. Spy Smasher.

Something Norm had told me about Ian's Bond novels. SMERSH. It meant "death to spies."

I tightened my slippery grip, vowing to smash all the spies in the world and heaved my weight one last time, causing the belt to work itself free and carry me to the window's ledge.

Minutes later, I was in and fumbled my way through a dark room to a darker corridor and down a flight of faintly creaking stairs, while trying to work my belt back into my pants. I saw and heard no one.

I finally reached the inside of the front entrance, picked up a dusty umbrella from a stand, and fought to control a sneeze. I didn't have a lot of time to hunt around for a better weapon, but the umbrella was almost as sturdy as a Louisville slugger, so I decided to become a swinger.

When I opened the door, I took the surprised guard from behind and hit a homer to the side of his head. The guard's rifle clattered to the street and skidded along the gutter. He went down, too, but not out.

I back-peddled, preparing to take another swing, just as he reached into the top of his right boot and pulled out a stubby bayonet. His eyes locked on mine, and we played stare-down for a good two seconds. Where the hell were my pals when I needed them?

I backed farther away, shrugging out of my jacket and draping it over my left forearm.

The knife flashed toward my face. I raised my arm and caught the blade in the folds.

The guard pulled back and scanned the sidewalk for his firearm. I swung at him again, trying to knock him down, or at least position him away from the rifle.

The knife sliced at my face again and bit into the umbrella's wooden staff and fabric. We both twisted our weapons and I lost. But the umbrella's awkward shape and extra weight threw the guard's arm off balance and I moved in to grab his left shoulder and spin him around to where Walt rose up and cracked him in the head with a paving stone.

The guard slid to the ground, and I jerked a thumb up and panted, "You're out."

CHAPTER 19

W e silently collected our prize and pulled it inside the annex, closing the entrance as a tower clock rang out the half hour. I kept the rifle.

Ian helped Walt truss up the guard's hands and feet with electric wires torn from a couple of floor lamps. At one point, the man came to his senses and started spouting a lot of German gibbety-gook, like *"Kimo sabe I stanford jolley clu gulager."*

I said, "I'm sorry, Donald, but I can't understand a word you're saying," and clunked him in the head with the rifle stock. I could tell that Walt enjoyed that, chuckling under his breath while he stuffed a thousand-year-old antimacassar into our captive's mouth and secured it with a curtain cord.

"So they call you the Grey Seal, huh?" I said. "You devil."

He laid a finger under his nose and scratched his missing mustache. "Mum's the word, and my head still hurts, but let's go find Poole."

෴

She was a modestly-dressed woman with gray hair and soft brown eyes. And she wasn't all there when we found her tied to a lion-clawed, wooden chair in a back room upstairs on the third floor. They had deprived her of sleep or given her dope, perhaps both. She was gagged with a scarf tied round her head, which was fortunate, because otherwise she'd have screamed bloody murder upon seeing us.

Ian tried to explain who were. Both he and Walt seemed to recognize her from past encounters. I too felt perhaps I'd seen her before. She had that kind of a face. Wrinkled, thin and a little dazed.

The room they'd held her in was the kind of office I'd seen in hundreds of movies from the 1930s. Heavy draperies covering high windows. Massive oaken desk with pen and pencil set, French phone and a green shaded desk lamp.

A few paintings on the walls displayed landscapes with rivers and green fields running to forever. I wished we were.

"Is she going to be able to walk?" Fleming asked, while Walt loosened her bonds.

"I think so." The film-maker directed his next statement to the woman: "Try and stand."

She came to her feet and tipped gently into my arms. Her gray eyes searched mine and seemed to find what she wanted. "Water?" she asked.

"Here, Penny," Walt said, finding a glass and pitcher on a stand beside a huge floor-standing radio from the 'twenties. She drank and sat back down. I took the empty glass from her shaking hand and noticed two syringes and a few small medical bottles of clear liquid setting on a nearby table. She had obviously been drugged and was now half delirious.

From over behind the massive desk, Fleming said, "The game changes again."

I raised my voice. "When does this damn game end?"

"When the West hand knows what the East hand is doing," the writer replied.

"And when is that?"

Walt answered, moving over to join Ian at the desk, "I think you know the answer, Stan," he said offhandedly.

"You're still not telling me everything, are you?"

He appeared to begin to answer, when Fleming looked up from the folder of papers he had been reading and remarked, "This is worse than I ever suspected."

"What is it now?" I asked, resting a reassuring hand on Agent Penny Poole's frail shoulder.

Ian held up a thin portfolio of dark brown leather. A few eight-by-ten glossy photographs dribbled onto the desktop. "Projekt GoldenHarz," he read from a document in his hands while Walt picked up the fallen photos. "Or as we'd say, Project Goldenheart. It's a weapon site in East Germany, about fifty kilometers, or thirty miles, north of here, near a small town of Vogelsang."

"Yes." Poole sighed next to me. "The Russians have rockets hidden there—against the arms agreement—pointed at England."

There was an urgent tone in her voice. I bent down to study her. "Rockets? You mean like V-2 rockets?"

She blinked, trying to hold me in focus. "No."

"No," Walt agreed, looking up from the papers held in Ian's hand. "They're missiles with thermo-nuclear warheads."

"Are you telling me," I asked, rushing over to study the documents, "that the Russians have nukes in Germany? Pointed at England?"

"We have to stop this," Fleming said.

"This is written in German," I charged.

"I can read it. But you see clearly from the photographs."

I tried to make sense of an aerial view of what could have been either a weapons depot or a housing development spread out near a river and a couple of lighter colored patches, intersected by straight lines that must have been highways.

"That's the warhead storage area and missile base," Ian said, pointing with a blunt finger. He then indicated an almost perfectly formed pentagonal shape in the middle of one of the gray areas. "That's the launch pad."

"Wait," I said, easing into the chair behind the desk. "Let me sit down."

"We have to get this information out to the West," Walt said, clearly astonished, "or they will threaten all of Europe."

"Nuclear missiles with a range that could strike and destroy London," Fleming said.

"Just—just wait," I said. "Let me get this straight. The Soviets have A-bombs trained on London. Is this why you needed to be here all along, Ian? To find proof of this threat?"

"H-bombs, more likely," Walt corrected.

"Same difference," I shot back. "This can't be true. Can it?"

"It is very true," Poole said, leaning earnestly toward us from her chair across the room.

"So, if it's true," I went on, "it would be like having nuclear missiles hidden, say, in Cuban bunkers, threatening to blast America into a...a..."

"Radioactive wasteland," Walt said.

"Wait," I said for the third time. "Let me think. Even if this is a hoax—"

"It's not," Fleming said. "This is the proof." He held the portfolio up at eye level. "Poole is right. We have got to get this story out to the West, where it can be dealt with in a proper manner by trained professionals."

"Once word gets out," I said, "they'll *have* to back down. Won't they?"

"Or they'll fire the things and start World War III," Walt said.

"They wouldn't dare. We'd retaliate and destroy them, ten to one. Wouldn't we?"

"Not if they strike first."

Mr. P had taught me to stay with a case until the end. Just being nosey or curious wasn't a good reason to be a detective. That almost never paid off, except in the movies. It was like drawing to an inside straight.

I tried to figure out what I was trying to figure out. I wasn't a fresh, young PI any more, like when I'd first started in the business with Mr. P. I was approaching middle-age and now knew that I wanted to do something that actually mattered and be more than just another hard-luck PI. If we succeeded getting this information out to the West, lives would be saved.

I'd missed World War II, because I too young. And then due to my bum shoulder, I'd missed the Korean conflict. All I had now was the Cold War. Maybe what I really wanted was to work a case that was bigger than anything Mr. P had ever handled.

I owed it to him to carry the tradition forward into

the second half of the twentieth century. Or maybe I was still fooling myself. The truth was that most of the time, I didn't know what I wanted and I let others decide things for me, like a pawn.

'*God, you're depressing,*' my dark side said.

No wonder I joked around so much. If I didn't, I'd be dead. And then where would I be? Probably just drinking cold beer in Akron.

I crossed back over to assist the woman by pouring another glass of water. Joyful participation in the sorrows of the workplace.

"It's too important to risk treating as a hoax," I said. "It *has* to be the Soviet's hidden gambit."

"But if we take these documents, they'll know that we know," Walt answered.

"It doesn't matter," Ian insisted. "We've got to take it."

"And we've got to get out of here," I stated. "Before Miss Russian Pegleg finds out that we've escaped."

"Then this is the first place she'll go, to secure her control over Poole," Walt concluded.

"I say, we leave now and take Poole and the documents with us," Ian directed.

"You've covered this part of the world for years," Walt said to Ian: "Can't you get us out?"

"All of my contacts here are long gone," the writer replied. "Except—"

I headed for the door. "While you guys figure it out,

I'm going down and check on the guard. And liberate his belt."

eↄeↄ

That wasn't all we liberated that night.

We found a suit of clothing in a closet to help disguise Agent Penny Poole. And, in addition to the guard's rifle, we appropriated his cap and boots.

"Can they really expect to hit London with a missile?" I asked Fleming.

"Two weeks ago, they aimed one at the moon and hit it. Imagine," he went on, "somewhere in the Black Forest, the whole of a green field slides back to reveal the dark mouth of a great subterranean bunker. The tip of a rocket emerges. First there's a trickle of steam from the rocket exhausts and then a great belch of flame, and slowly the rocket climbs off its launching pad on its way directly at the heart of your nation."

It sounded so vivid, I thought that I'd seen it on *You Asked For It*.

By now, the Vopos could be searching for us. We had to get back with this portfolio of information. Then the commies might withdraw the nukes for fear of recriminations, or a pre-emptive strike. I Felt like Errol Flynn in *Desperate Journey*, only this was desperate-*er*.

We needed to make contact with Fleming's agent back at the Lenin Hotel. So while darkness and patrol cars still dominated the streets, we made our way across the broad, two-lane boulevard, halfway between the Berlin State Opera and the Russian Embassy. Taking time to hide the rifle inside a trash can in a dark alley, we walked into the lobby and searched for our man.

I yawned so hard to relieve the tension that I almost cracked my jaw.

"Stay alert," Ian said. "There he is."

Fleming left our group and walked over to the newsstand counter where he had a brief exchange with a weather-faced male attendant who looked a lot like Spencer Tracy. I casually followed along to lend protection, if needed. Ian purchased a newspaper and a packet of chewing gum, paying for them with one of his odd British coins. The attendant gave him back his change, including a key and a slip of paper.

The German chewing gum tasted like German chewing gum. I discreetly deposited it and the wrapper in a pot of sand beside the elevator.

The four of us filed into the cramped space and Ian pressed the button for the third floor. As the doors slid shut, I saw a Vopo enter the lobby and begin looking around.

Using the key to enter room 303, we eased Poole onto the bed, where she mumbled her thanks, closed her eyes, and began to breathe evenly.

"Is she going to make it?" I asked.

"She'd better," Walt said.

"We can't stay here," I told them. "The state police will be searching and find us."

"Is anybody else hungry?" Walt said.

Ian went over to the room's telephone. "I'm almost out of cigarettes."

"Good thing," I said. "You're not going to call room service, are you?"

He began dialing. "What do you take me for?"

"You guys are starting to go vague on me again," I warned.

"Hello, Cork Travel Bureau. This is Manchester," he said into the instrument. "Are you there, M?"

I watched Walt for a sign. The sign was to relax.

Fleming went on, "If you think someone is listening, say something with the word Tuesday in it." He waited and then nodded, consulting what looked like a train schedule in the newspaper and giving instructions for our transport out of the country, while I again checked on the woman's condition. She murmured something in her sleep, but otherwise lay quiet.

Fleming he handed the phone to me. "It's Molly and your boy, Norman. They'll arrange for us to get back to West Berlin, but we've got to tell them where to meet us. Walter, my man, can you locate the best spot?"

I accepted the receiver and put it to my ear, while Walt flipped the pages of a worn phonebook and consulted with Ian. "Testing, testing," I said into the phone. "Is this thing on?"

"This is SS3 to SS1," Norm said. "Over." He was doing his Captain Midnight Secret Squadron signaling routine.

Walter, my man, came over and began pointing to a place on the map in the phonebook. Ian was with him, watching closely.

"Hold on," I said to Norm. "I've got one for you."

Walt tapped the map and I tilted my head to see where he was indicating.

"You reach the...Kurfurstendamm station about a quarter to five. Read a magazine and you're in...Frankfurt, alive. Get me?"

"Dinner in the diner. Nothing could be finer," Norm answered.

I nodded to Walt and Ian. "Good."

They seemed relieved.

"*Klaatu Barada Nikto*," Norm said and the line went dead.

I caught Fleming still studying me.

"What is it now?" I asked, settling into an over-stuffed chair and trying to massage the pain from my stiff leg.

"I can't figure you out, Wade, old boy" he said, lighting a cigarette from the stub of one that Walt had given him. "As a writer, I'm constantly observing the way other people act. Sometimes you seem to stand outside of everything that's happening around you, and other times you're in the thick of it all."

I transferred the massaging action to the lump at the base of my neck. "A man you can't kid is a man you can't trust," I quoted. "But it's probably just due to my thick head, old boy."

"We need to get a truck out of here," Walt said.

Fleming winced at the comment. "Language, please, Walter."

"What?" I said. "He was speaking English."

"I know." Ian sighed. "And he's right. We need to find transportation to our pickup spot. Let's go."

I unsettled out of the overstuffed chair and we all went.

CHAPTER 20

It was the easiest part of our escape plan. We hired a taxi. In a culture of fear and duplicity, everyone in East Berlin was out for himself, even at this late hour.

Our driver glumly accepted the high-denomination Marks that Fleming shoved at him. I gave the cabman the rest of the pack of gum, while we piled in. Walt retrieved the rifle without a word and set it in the back seat next to Agent Poole.

After a twenty-minute ride, we were dropped off in the northern part of the city about three-quarters of a mile from our intended destination. Out here, away from the lights of the metropolitan area, the night huddled in closer.

We made our way down a pocked road, past distant

houses and a few out buildings, between weed-infested lots—three men god-fathering an elderly woman. Somewhere behind us, a dog barked forlornly and then quieted down again, as we moved farther along.

"Still got that portfolio?" Walt asked Ian.

The writer patted his breast pocket.

"Still know where we're going?" I asked.

Ian stopped and I almost stumbled into him.

"I know this place," Fleming said, recognition softening his face. "We dug a communications tunnel not more than four hundred yards from here back in '52 to intercept Russian teleprinter cable traffic."

Agent Poole quietly sighed. "Yes."

Fleming started walking forward again. "And then it rained. Leaked into the cable line and they sent repair trucks out to fix the break."

"What happened?" I asked, adjusting my grip on the rifle.

"The Russians arrived with tommy guns," Ian continued, stepping around a large pot hole. "Most of us got out in time, but one chap died here."

"William Adams," Poole said.

Again Ian stopped, acting slightly dazed or amazed. We waited. "Yes, Adams. He took a bullet that was meant for me. I've never gotten over the guilt."

I could identify with the feeling and thought again of Max. "And you never will," I said.

We started moving again. The writer said, "We left a

sign in the tunnel for them to find. It read, 'You are now entering the British sector.'"

I had to laugh, quietly.

"Anyone have an aspirin?" Walt asked.

We came to a gravel drive that led back to a bombed out and abandoned Catholic church. A few bats from central casting fluttered overhead in the dim moonlight as we made our way around to the back to gather in a small, unkempt graveyard. A high stone wall enclosed us on three sides. I didn't like the feeling that came with this gothic location. Weather-worn inscriptions in old German on the headstones around us dated the graves as far back as 1540. It would have made a great new location at Walt's theme-park. Macabreland.

We shuffled over and stood by the weeds at the back wall, unhindered. The night air smelled of loam and dead flowers. There were other dead things all around us, but I tried not to think about that. I breathed in the cold night and decided it was an improvement over the smog back home, which was about the only thing I liked about the place.

"I think I hear an owl," Walt said, stretching his back.

"This is the very definition of a dead end," I told Ian. "How will we get out?"

"You'll see soon enough," the writer said.

An ugly thought struck me. "Oh, crap! Not the miserable sewers, I hope. That would be like hell."

"We're going the other way," Walt commented.

I decided to try a different tack. "I wonder if you know that your eyes change color slightly whenever you lie."

He looked at me like I was a comical sidekick. "Uh, you mean like Pinocchio, or something?"

"Or something." I went back to my previous query: "So where do we go from here?"

"I told you. We wait," Fleming answered, inserting a Player in his mouth. Then, probably imagining the cloud of smoke it would create, he slid it unlit back into the pack and placed the pack back into his pocket.

I scraped my fingernails along the stubble on my chin and noticed the similar fuzz sprouting on the dark faces of Ian and Walt. What a scruffy and wild bunch we were becoming. International intrigue could do that to you.

I wondered again about Ian Fleming. Here was a writer who had considerable experience with espionage. He wrote about the subject in his fiction, but acted as if it were his true calling. A spy whose cover story was spy stories. As improbable as it seemed, in this business of double-double agents, it almost made sense. Almost as much as a cartoonist/movie producer who worked for the FBI/CIA.

It was clear that both of these men had more than one career and more than one cause that drove them. Fleming probably never left his country's secret service and had contacts all over the world. For all I knew, some other guy ghostwrote his Bond novels. Probably Shakespeare's ghost.

Walt, on the other hand, was first and foremost a businessman. But, at some point in his past, he'd been recruited into his other guise and its web of intrigue. Now, he wouldn't, or couldn't get out. I wondered why, especially when he had so much going for him elsewhere in his life. Rescuing Poole almost seemed like a personal quest on his part.

I considered the woman again and her possible past. Was there an old romance there between them? She was the right age to have been Walt's lover or mistress in the past. And they *did* exchange significant glances from time to time.

I noticed that the left sleeve of my coat had a three-inch gash in it and tried to backtrack through the trail of events to review what little I knew of her. An American agent during the war. Undercover in some role during the filming of *Ben Hur*. Supposedly, she knew of another agent who'd died during filming.

Both Ian and Walt had known she was involved with spy plane operations over the Soviet Union, channeling information back to the US. The Russians had found out about the flights crossing high over their border and taken her captive. Was she a pawn, or a queen?

If she was on the side of the Communists, then the Goldenheart information was likely a hoax. But we couldn't take the chance of ignoring it. And both Walt and Ian acted as if the threat was heart-attack real. So, what *was* the truth? And would I ever know it, assuming that I ever saw it within this double-dealing business?

I realized I'd just gone around in a mental circle.

I stamped my feet to keep warm, or maybe because I was so frustrated with half-truths and half-answers. Checking my watch and doing a quick calculation, I realized that it was 9 p.m. Saturday evening back home and I'd just missed the season premiere of *Perry Mason*.

"They're coming," Walt said.

I stamped my feet again and blew out a cloud of steaming breath. I could hear a car approaching, but couldn't tell from which direction. I moved closer to the wall, still holding the rifle, and the other members of my group automatically followed. There was no way to climb over, dig under, or blast through.

Headlights swept closer from the side of the church. The car's tires crunched the gravel.

We all ducked for what scant cover we could find, trapped in an enclosure of stone, surrounded by tombs. My mind stupidly flashed on another grave site I'd visited earlier in the year, Chandler's grave. A spotlight flared from the approaching car, pinning us in its yellow-white beam.

The car's engine stopped.

We huddled behind the ancient tombstones.

"Raise your hands to the perpendicular," a voice

called out in English from behind the glare. "Or we will shoot."

I ran my tongue over my teeth and tasted accumulated scum.

Someone on the other side of the car said, "Lace fingers behind your head." I started to heft the rifle, but thought better of it, since I recognized the second voice as that of Nikkita Reed. "Put weapon down," she commanded. "And stand straight."

Again I looked around, this time with the help of the vehicle's dazzling searchlight, but there was still no way out. Our two attackers came forward, carrying side arms. I let the rifle fall to my feet.

"I told you that we should have stayed with them, instead of going to that meeting," Yuri said.

He was chiding Nikkita, confident now that they had the upper hand.

"You were one who wanted to meet with head of MVD," the woman replied. "Always looking for a promotion or to expand your influence."

"And you are just as ambitious to advance your career," he answered.

"You don't need us to work out your differences," I said. "We'll just be running along now."

"Stop or I'll shoot!" Yuri barked. They were backlit by their car's headlights. Perfect targets.

"There's a tracking device in the portfolio, isn't there?" Ian said. "I should have checked."

"Yes, you should have," Nikkita said. "You western-ers are such naive fools."

"Isn't that a line from one of your books, Ian?" I asked.

"Give me credit, Wade. I don't write that low level of pulp fiction."

"Shut up!" Yuri shouted, louder this time, stepping closer. "The world will soon learn that the great western filmmaker and the famous Commander Fleming have de-fected to the East."

"So that's your plan now," I said. "You're pretty confident."

"And with good reason," Nikkita replied, also mov-ing forward. "Soon I'll have revenge for death of my brother and our side will have everything it seeks to con-firm your U-2 flights." Her eyes were dark—and not from heavy makeup. "Bat even more important, with Pro-ject Goldenherz, Mother Russia will reward us with high honors, elevated position, and great riches."

"So, you're both capitalists, after all," Walt com-mented.

Nikkita smirked. "The American dream."

"There is nothing you can do to stop us," Yuri de-clared. In his zeal, he cast around for the right threat. Then he found it. "We will bury you behind the Iron Cur-tain."

At gunpoint in a graveyard. A terrific title. What was I thinking?

"Get on your knees, now," Yuri said.

A loud roaring noise thundered up from the other side of the wall behind us.

"This is it," Walt called out. "They're coming."

The sound grew louder.

"What are they doing?" I yelped. "Drilling from China?"

The roar increased, sounding more and more like a helicopter. Yuri and Nikkita backed away.

A wind kicked up, sending dead leaves and dirt into my eyes, as a huge disk rose over the top of the wall.

It hovered there, like a flying saucer. A man stood on top of it, behind a railing that ran all around the upper edge of the thing. The giant horizontal fan wavered and tilted slightly, slipping over the confining wall to float to the ground with the sound of a thousand lawn mowers.

The two Red agents retreated in the direction of their car.

I took a chance and grabbed the rifle back up, firing it at our attackers.

Walt didn't hesitate to drag Poole toward the hover device. They climbed under the railing and stood next to the operator, gesturing for us to follow. Ian turned to be sure I wasn't frozen in my tracks.

'*Holy shit!*' the Noir Man said.

I fired again, but the soviet weapon jammed. Yuri and Nikkita stayed behind their car, sending a few bullets in our general direction, but striking nothing. Fleming yanked my good shoulder. We stumbled aboard even as the thing began to rise again off the ground.

I stared down through the tight grillwork and saw the earth moving away under my feet and the whirling blades.

Shots wanged off the metal enclosure and the tone of the engine shifted. We rose higher, dipped, swerving due to the extra weight, and glided past the top of the wall into the night sky and no-man's land.

The pilot wrestled with the controls. He wore US Navy blues and slumped to the left while the platform went to the right. Then he slumped to the deck-work, still holding fast to the steering assembly with an upraised hand. Blood poured from his chest.

Ian gathered the man to him. I reached over and tried to correct our tilting flight.

"Can you fly a chopper?" Walt yelled at me.

"I usually fly an X-15," I said, biting my sore lip to keep from giggling.

"Then get us to the train station," Ian commanded.

"Ten-four," I shouted back. Nobody caught my error in jargon. They were all too busy hanging on for dear life.

CHAPTER 21

Anyone know how to land this thing?" I shouted. They were all clustered together, clutching onto the railing that circled the parameter of the weird craft.

"Ian," I hollered, grasping the flight controls. But the writer was busy stuffing papers into his coat pockets and jettisoning the portfolio with its tracking sensor over the side.

"Take it up," Walt commanded.

"How, dammit?"

The giant fan beneath our feet growled. We tilted more to the left and the wind tore at our clothing. Poole was slumped to her knees between the two men. The pilot's body slid to the edge, one arm dangling over the side.

I held fast to the controls and spread my legs wide, trying desperately to hold myself erect.

We had passed some thirty feet beyond the wall as the whining craft eased up and over a flatbed truck which must have delivered the hover craft to the site on the western side of the church's walled enclosure.

The horizon tilted again, this time to the right.

I worked the throttle and shoved an acceleration lever forward. We whizzed up above a small stand of trees. I could see a road down below that fed into an empty highway.

Something went crack and a round from a firearm behind and below us buzzed past my ear. Another bullet zinged into the underside of the blades spinning beneath us.

I shifted my weight, as if that could help steer the monster, and took us lower, accelerating along to the crossroads.

"Take it more to the right," Walt yelled. "Near those buildings."

We were level again, scooting along the highway, surfing at a good speed away from our attackers.

The pilot almost slid off the metal platform, but Ian caught him by the back of his collar and heaved the poor man farther aboard.

"Keep going," Walt cried as we dipped down at a tremendous speed.

I fought the controls to keep us airborne.

"I can't hold him," Ian said.

I glanced back in time to see the pilot's body roll and cast free into the night.

"Shit," was my single reply through clinched teeth.

"Up, up," Walt shouted. "You've got it now."

"I don't want it!"

"More to starboard. That way. Up, up!"

I shifted my stance and caught sight of the glow in the eastern sky. My arms were beginning to cramp from holding the steering column and urging the crazy craft onward.

Walt shouted into my ear, "That way."

I looked where he was pointing and saw three rows of railroad tracks stretching into the countryside.

We soared past and over more trees and a couple of rural wooden buildings. A herd of dairy cows scattered in all directions as we flew down and along the rails.

"Take the one that goes south," Ian directed.

The three tracks below began to separate to their designated destinations. I had no idea which of the three lead south. Then I got my bearings from the rising sun and we sped along, clipping the treetops.

In the far distance, I saw the long dark snake of a train curving away from us, around a bend. I eased the controls in that direction and the whirly-fan came nearer to the train and its trailing cloud of steam.

Ian's voice rose above the motor's howl. "Down, down."

Did he want us to hit the train?

We hovered above a crawling line of boxcars. Walt came along the railing, hand over hand, to help with the controls.

"Leave me alone," I told him. "I've got the hang of it now."

He pointed down at an empty flatcar speeding below that seemed as big as a paperback book.

The sun was high enough now that I could clearly see the idiotic thing that he wanted done.

I gave him my sternest expression.

He nodded and pointed down again with more authority.

"You're totally nuts!" I declared.

The train under us must have been traveling at a rate of thirty miles an hour. That meant we were also skimming along at least as fast above it.

I shook my head, ignoring the pain and his command. A thick cloud of steam filled my throat and eyes.

Walt and I struggled over the controls for a couple of seconds and the craft banged down on the wooden surface of the speeding train. We bounced back up eight or nine feet and almost tipped into the back of the rear boxcar.

The throttle slipped from my grip. Walt caught it and the hovercraft banged again onto the deck of the moving car.

The roar of the fan scaled down. The craft skidded

along the wooden surface, sending up splinters and grit.

We were almost down, but grinding our way more and more toward the edge of the speeding flatcar.

I yanked Walt's arm, hoping to drag us back to center. A screeching cry of metal against metal bore into my ears.

The craft bounced again and thumped into the back of the forward boxcar, settling into place like a pinball into a slot.

Ian and Poole fell on their backs, jerked free of the railing by the impact.

The engine shut down like a dying siren.

"Off, off," Walt ordered, while trees and telephone lines flashed past on both sides.

"I am *never* doing *that* again," I swore.

Behind me, the British writer said, "Me too neither," as the train picked up speed and plunged into the black mouth of a long tunnel.

The roar of the train's exhaust reverberated like a hundred bass drums. Soon a tiny circle of light materialized ahead in the darkness and quickly grew wider, as the train burst into the bright sunlight with a noise like thunder.

"We're not climbing over top of any freight cars to get to a coach," I screamed. "Poole will never make it."

"Don't worry," Walt called back. "This is not an express. It's a steam-driven local, making limited stops. The next one should come up sometime soon."

Ian pulled the rail schedule from his pocket. It almost whipped out of his hand, as he said, "We can get off then and buy tickets to Frankfurt."

The long-chassed locomotive panted with the labored breath of a dragon dying of asthma in the October air. I was reminded of Walter Mitty's *ta-pakita-pakita*.

"I'll contact the military and report the location of the hover platform and the pilot's body," Walt said.

"What about Norman and Molly O'Dee?" I asked.

"They should already be onboard in one of the carriages, waiting for us to show up," Ian replied.

"Please." Poole's breath wavered in her throat. "Don't say 'Up.'"

The train slowed its pace and we pulled into a station where we disembarked clumsily. The plan was to use some of the diamonds to pay our fare, but we still had enough Marks to satisfy the conductor without drawing much suspicion. Ian handled the language barrier. We had succeeded in getting away, but we weren't out of Germany yet.

ℭↄℭↄ

"What the hell happened?" Molly's accent had slipped.

She had her hair done up in one of those French twists. We were gathered and seated in what was once called a private drawing room with curtained windows facing the speeding countryside. It was like something out of the nineteenth century. Not exactly the Orient Express, but a worn-down fancy conveyance with cushioned seats, pull-down beds, and a private lavatory.

Norm looked quiet better, but he still depended on Karloff's cane to get around. He sat quietly for once beside Poole who still appeared exhausted, but pleased to have escaped confinement.

We described our Berlin adventures and Nikkita Reed. Molly had heard of her, especially when I mentioned the sickle-shaped scar, but knew nothing of her prosthetic weapons cache.

"That Hiller Flying Platform is a definite E-ticket ride," Walt concluded. "I'll have to speak with the military about getting something like that at my theme park."

The train howled, clicking off a mile a minute, skimming along the tracks.

"After this, I need to retire from the espionage business," Walt said,

"Amen," Ian said. "This is much more than any of us planned on."

"There was a plan?" I asked.

"There were a couple of them," Walt replied.

"None of which either of you told me about," I complained. "Level with me, Walt. What are you not telling us?"

"About what, precisely? The hovercraft?"

Ian broke in with, "We had Molly set up the rescue

with your military service as a contingency before we left West Berlin."

"There," I charged, "right there. You two didn't tell me about that, or your true connection with our government."

Walt shrugged. "I'm a resource and I have resources."

"Then what's your role in all of this, uh, caper? Hell, what's my role? Start back at the beginning."

He barely suppressed a sigh. "It started a long time back with *Victory Through Air Power*."

"That's too far back," I said.

"Just how old do you think I am?" he asked.

"Not as old as I feel," Norman said.

"You know that I'm not young anymore," Walt went on, "but I still have to help defend democracy."

"Yeah, I know. Liberty and justice for all. But why here? Why now?"

Fleming searched his pockets for his missing cigarette holder and then gave up. "We're on the front lines of a cold war that could heat up any minute, Wade. Sometimes the less said, the better for all. You've seen that."

Walt handed him the last of his crumpled pack of filter-tipped L&Ms. "I could never have flown that hover platform or climbed across to that annex, or escaped from the East without your strength and skills, Stan."

I wanted so much to respond to this compliment by simply punching his lights out. "From now on, I need to know everything, or I won't be able to trust either of you."

Molly reached out and touched my sliced sleeve from where she sat. "What, pray tell, are ya complainin aboot? Ya should be happy that we rescued Poole and got oot of Berlin in one piece."

"Not to mention," Ian added, "we've gained proof of the Soviet's nuclear threat to Western Europe."

Walt shook his head, amused by something. "You flew that thing like Hotshot Charlie."

"I don't know if that's good or bad."

"We walked away, didn't we?" Ian said.

Outside, a clanging bell shifted down the Doppler as we soared past.

"This spy stuff is way over my head," I said to Ian.

"In time," he said, "you'll find that it's *kinderspiele*. Kid games."

Walt added, "Just let your conscience be your guide."

'*Slug him*,' the Noir Man said. I clinched my fists.

"You could blame it all on the IGY," Norm said.

Knowing full well that there's no stopping Norman when he got into lecture mode, I still had to ask, "The IGY? Another secret spy organization?"

"The International Geophysical Year. Teams of scientists are going out all over the world this year from the Arctic to the Equator in an all-out effort to find what makes our planet tick."

"Before it blows up, eh?" I countered. "That's no excuse for us running around the continent like the Rover Boys, doing and saying whatever we like."

"I agree in principle, but think of the alternative," Ian said.

"Aye," Molly commented, "Think what'll likely happen in the future, if we doone act now."

I watched a fly crawl across the window. "Well, at least, we should advise the authorities."

"We have, Stan. And we shall again, soon enough," Walt tried to assure me. "Timing is everything in these situations."

"In the end, we're going to need all the help we can get, and that's always the best time to explain everything to the authorities," Ian said. "Or, at least explain some part of it all."

Norman reached into his many-pocketed vest and came up with something in his hand. "Want your key back?"

Walt glanced at Ian, who shot a look in Molly's direction.

I accepted the key, wrapped in a scrap of paper, with a slight flourish.

"So what's in the safety deposit box?" Norm asked innocently.

It was my turn to be mysterious. "I'll tell you—someday."

CHAPTER 22

The train continued along the steel tracks of the Deutsche Bundesbahn, huffing and wheezing toward Frankfurt, while the members of our little Team Bay City kept still, quiet, and to ourselves. We had left our bags back at the hotel and the few possessions we'd carried to the church graveyard were now also far behind. The train stopped at three stations along the way. Each time, we waited on the alert, while the whistle sounded a mournful *whooo-whu-whu-whu* call.

Passengers got off and climbed on to hang out the windows and jabber at the thin crowd below. Then the conductor would pick up the iron pedestal beside the carriage and climb with it onto the train, raising a hand to the engineer and fireman to start.

Finally we reached Frankfurt, around eleven a.m.

The Hauptbahnhof train station was a dead-end terminus with a nineteenth-century glass-and-iron construction from the Industrial Revolution full of green copper figures representing steam power and electricity. From here, we would have to travel by bus across the border into France.

While Molly continued to tend to Norman and Poole, Walt, Ian, and I came out onto the station platform. Military guards of several nations mingled around us. Most of them were from West Germany.

I saw a few American uniforms, identifying our boys on leave from a nearby base. We were relatively safe here, almost out of the country, but we remained cautious.

Ian went off to make a phone call. I purchased large German pretzels and half-dozen pickle-and-mayo sandwiches wrapped in wax paper from an elderly street merchant in a Tyrolean hat.

Walt conferred with several low-level members of the US Army who had come to retrieve the hover platform. "At least we proved that the prototype had more vector-thrust than originally planned," I overheard him tell them.

"The military is not happy with the way you abused its valuable equipment," a young sergeant advised. "You'll have a hellova time explaining it all when you get back."

At the end of the station platform, a car drew up and

two people I didn't like got out, working their way through the crowd—Nikkita and Yuri.

I urgently tugged at Walt's sleeve and turned us away from our pursuers, who must have driven at top speed to have intercepted us here.

Walt handed me all but one of the pretzels and shouldered his way past a middle-aged man and wife with three children in tow.

I eased back in the direction of our train, hoping to be as inconspicuous and uninteresting as a trash receptacle.

Yuri drew nearer, searching. Walt hunched down onto a bench outside a ticket office and stuffed the last of his salted snack into his mouth, as Kaminski stepped right past him.

Ian took that unfortunate moment to come back toward the train. Nikkita spotted him before I could give warning. The woman gestured in Fleming's direction. I moved behind a pillar, trying to stay out of view.

Yuri joined his comrade next to Ian. Quiet words were passed in German and Ian's face paled a bit. I tried to dream up something to do to stop them, as they began to move off together toward the waiting car.

Walt got up and followed, stopping to speak with his army contacts. The soldiers listened, looked, and then eased over to confront the pair of commies and the writer.

More words in German were passed around. Stern, accusing words. The young sergeant drew his sidearm and now it was Yuri's turn to pale. The soldiers called for reinforcements and a small crowd had begun to form. The fresh-faced sergeant reached into Yuri's coat pocket and pulled out a pistol and a worn leather wallet.

From out of the crowd, the middle-aged father of the three children rushed over. More German-speak and then Ian stepped away from his captors, obviously relieved.

It was like watching a silent movie. Yuri seemed stunned. Nikkita simmered with controlled aggression and wrath. The young soldier handed the wallet to the father, who checked its contents and pointed accusingly at the two Red agents.

The army man said something like, "Consider yourself under arrest, Mein Herr," and they all moved in the direction of the station's entrance.

I almost dropped the sandwiches as Walt met Ian and brought him back in my direction. I stammered, "Did— did you just pick that guy's pocket and plant his wallet on Kaminski?"

Walt smiled with unrestrained pride. "Guilty as charged."

I stared again at the soldier and figured out who he was. Our pursuers where lead quietly past us. Nikkita's eyes bore into mine. Her face was as red as an exit sign.

I felt elated. "This is *our* hidden gambit," I said to her. Then my accumulated frustration ran over and I couldn't stop myself from wise cracking, "Add the letter 'A' to my first name and it spells Satan."

Walt laughed as the Reds were hustled away. "Their diplomatic authority will have them free very soon, so we need to keep moving. By the way, did you recognize the young army sergeant?"

My eyes tracked over to the departing soldier, who turned and gave us a half salute. "Yep. He looks pretty good in a uniform."

We walked to the train to collect our teammates.

"Who is he?" Ian inquired, accepting a sandwich. "One of your legion of undercover men?"

"Pretzel?" I offered. "Elvis...Pretzel?"

A boarding announcement clamored out in three languages, covering Fleming's response.

Minutes later, we all caught the bus that would take us across the Rhine River to the border.

eↄeↄ

By 1 p.m., we were standing at a typical wayside checkpoint, under a white canopy marked with a turquoise *Touring* sign, listening to distant church bells.

A police official in a dark green uniform with dull-black pistol holster at his belt barely glanced at my passport. He snapped it shut and handed it to the bus driver, who handed it to me.

The man saluted and I gave him a thumbs-up. It was the only gesture I could think of that wouldn't offend.

Then we were back on the bus and across the border,

where we had to do the whole thing all over again in reverse. This time, we stood outside a façade of dour buildings and a dusty expanse of wooden counters, but no apparent armed guards. Just a few chickens pecking about and a few drab officials standing idly, unshaven, not even trying to look important. "*Passports. Douane.*"

Again, the bus bumped along the countryside. Hills rose and fell away. I glanced over at Walt. Between the hovercraft and the wallet-handoff gig, he had grown more impressive to me.

Scattered cottages, tilled fields, and pastures were blurred in a crawling panorama until we reached the outskirts of Strasbourg and wound our way around to what they called the Gare Centrale on the northwest corner of the city. Somewhere along the way, we had crossed a time zone and it was noon again, with more church bells marking the event.

This area of France had changed hands back and forth with Germany so many times in the last several hundred years that there were two names for everything here. French *choucroute* was the same as German *sauerkraut*, which of course was really steamed, sliced, and cooked cabbage. We abandoned our slow motorbus and transferred to a new French diesel-electric TransEurope Express train that gave a slap-happy whistle as we boarded and sped westward again.

There were no private carriages or drawing rooms on the TEE, just clean, efficient passenger-cars full of coach seats that faced forward or back, depending on how they were levered.

The six members of our team broke up into smaller groups to avoid seeming conspicuous. Norm and Molly found a discarded French-and-English guide book and were poring over it together, chatting like high-school kids on a senior-class trip.

Ian came forward to sit next to me among several rows of empty seats. "If you don't mind," he said, "I'd like to talk over something with you quietly."

I waited, watching out the window as a fairytale land of vineyards faded into the watercolor distance and half-timbered villages looked freshly-minted from *Snow White* or *Cinderella*. I reminded myself that all of it could be gone in a nuclear flash.

"Has Walt recruited you?" Fleming asked in hushed tones. "Or are you a lone hand? You seem very capable."

I waited some more. He and Walt had seemed so confident, cool, and sure that they were doing the right thing. It was a marvel, given the circumstances.

'*So many people have a hidden side,*' the Noir Man told me.

"How would you like to operate unofficially for the British Secret Service? On American soil, of course."

I raised my eyebrows for something to do. "Are you trying to recruit me to spy on my own country?"

"Well, let us call it a liaison. Her Majesty needs in-formation from a variety of sources, particularly in Hollywood. And some of our existing sources are becoming suspect."

I assumed he was talking about a person I knew, but instead he groused quietly about someone named Philby. I interrupted by asking, "Would the liaison include reporting on Walt's activities?"

"Whatever. Anything you found…interesting." He kept his voice low, like we were in church or a hospital room with a dying patient. "As you've seen, these are desperate times for all nations. Compensation would be placed into a numbered Swiss account, depending on the quality of information provided."

"Let me think about it," I said, looking back to where the others of our group sat, resting. "Okay, I've thought about it. No. In fact, as my old Pappy used to say, 'Hell, no.'" I cleared my throat. "It's not my line of work. Plus, I have a mean streak of honor in me. Comes from eating Wheaties."

Ian took it without blinking. "Very well," he said, getting up. "No harm done then. Let me know if you change your mind."

This entire affair had been as intricate and involved as an Arapaho Indian rug. Half the time, I didn't know up from down, as if I were in freefall. Boy, would I be glad to get back home.

The fast train sped along into a bowl of open land, flat and stony, where a river diverged into a network of rambling channels winding across hard barren ground broken by a few stunted trees. It had been a full twenty-four hours, and now everything conspired to make me sleep.

The hasty metal gallop of the wheels, the hypnotic swoop of the telegraph wires, the drowsy metallic clatter of the couplings, the occasional moan of the whistle clearing the way.

As we neared the city of Nancy, Walt and Fleming stayed with our two invalids, and Molly motioned for me to come out into the corridor with her, wanting to know more about the nukes and Goldenharz.

I gave her the little I knew, plus some of my misgivings about the whole affair. I wanted to test her reaction.

She patted my elbow. "Be strong and courageous. Deuteronomy 31:6."

"Sort of hard to do when nukes are involved."

"'Tis unbelievable," she said. "Arr ya certain we can entirely trust yer friend, Walter?"

I looked deeply into her eyes. "You're not really Irish, are you?"

The lids fluttered involuntarily. "How—did you—"

"Your accent slips when you recite Bible verses. Why do you do that?"

She led me into the companion-way between the two carriages. The rhythmic rattle of the rails and couplings surrounded us in a light breeze.

"I was imprisoned for six months in Helsinki with nothing but the good book to occupy my mind." She glanced up to see if I bought it. "Are ya goin ta tell on me, Stanley?"

I resigned myself to going along with her nonsense. "Nah, I'm pretty good at keeping secrets. It's all part of being a private—"

She nodded. "Aye."

The door of the other car slid open with a rush and Nikkita stepped out gracefully, waving a handgun. "You capitalists think that your great number of goods equals the greater good."

I wished I'd said that. In my line of business, I tend not to use the term "flatfoot," but that's how I felt then. I held onto the brass guardrail on the side of the coach near my head as the train swayed slightly and the commie woman addressed Molly about being some sort of cat burglar or jewel thief. Another persona? I watched the gun and decided that I needed a secret identity, since everybody else seemed to have one.

The train began to screech and slow as we came into the town of Nancy and neared a stone viaduct. The couplings beneath our feet groaned and nuzzled each other above the blurring tracks.

I couldn't figure a safe way to get the gun away from Nikkita, so I asked her, "When you pass a mirror, is there a reflection?"

The scar on her cheekbone reddened. The finger on the trigger whitened. At last, she had found the perfect opportunity to exact revenge for her brother's death.

"Careful now," I advised everyone, but Molly grunted, unladylike, and grabbed me, tumbling us off the train, down a high, scrub-filled embankment.

A bush branch smacked me across the eyes. We rolled, holding onto each other as long as we could. Then I lost my grip and breath and slammed into the base of a tree. Molly summersault clumsily into a thicket. Our train crossed the viaduct and vanished behind an imposing edifice of red sandstone, slipping farther into the city without us.

Her quick action had both jeopardized and saved our lives. We got up, dusted off, and climbed back up to the gleaming rails. My shoulder popped, but I kept quiet about it. Molly swore in three languages and dabbed at a bleeding scratch on her cheek, as we followed the tracks into the southwest side of what she pronounced as "None-see."

"Somehoo," I mocked, limping. "I dinna think it matterrs mooch, lassie."

She threw a cinder at me.

Twenty minutes later, under the hot afternoon sun, we caught sight of the express again, just as it was leaving the station. I hollered and waved my arms, but the train ignored me and picked up speed until it was completely out of sight. If I'd had a hat, I would have thrown it on the ground and stomped it flat. Instead, I fumed and looked around the station for some way to catch up with Walt and the others, before it was too late.

Molly pointed to long-faced man sitting in a small convertible. "It's a Citroen DS," she said, "And it can get up to 120 kilometers on a straightaway."

She moved with determination toward the vehicle and I knew then that she intended to steal the car and chase the train.

Not seeing any alternative, I rattled the lose diamonds in my pocket and took out a few. I offered them to the man, pointing at his car.

"*Nous acheton le voiture*," Molly insisted. "*Vite, vite.*"

The man jumped out, without opening the car door, and handed her the keys.

"I'll drive," she continued, sliding behind the steering wheel.

I handed over the diamonds and hopped in, calling, "Go, Molly, go," as we kicked up gravel and a cloud of gray dust.

CHAPTER 23

We bounced along the slight embankment beside the railway tracks.

She wrenched the wheel to force the tires over the nearest rail. Straddling it, the little French car pounded on the crossties with bone-jarring repetition.

Suddenly, I saw the back end of the train against the hard-blue sky. A wail from the engine filled the air ahead of us. The long line of railcars slowed to take a bending upgrade slope in the tracks.

Molly gunned the motor and accelerated back onto the gravel roadway, the seat-cushions bucking violently under our butts.

We halved the distance between us and the train. Halved it again, until we were only ten feet behind.

I climbed across the seat into the back of the car,

preparing to try and jump as we pulled alongside of the speeding train. The empty observation deck on the back of the last car beckoned to me. Like an idiot, I reached out a hand to try and grasp the railing or a rung of the side ladder.

The racing car beneath me swerved at the last second to avoid hitting a telephone pole, and I almost fell sideways onto the jagged rocks.

Molly's long red hair whipped and tore at my face in the wind. We overtook the train again. She gunned the engine, and I seized the ladder rung and jumped.

My fingers slipped on the cold steel. Pain tore down my arm like fire. I fell roughly on my right hip and banged my head on the metal deck. I got my knees under me and then my feet.

Molly and the Citroen convertible were still thumping along beside the train. Less than fifty feet ahead, I saw a phone pole that was set closer than the others to the rail. There was no room for her to squeeze the car between it and the train.

I stretched out a hand and snagged a few wisps of her fluttering hair. It caught her attention and she leaned in my direction. I clutched at her collar, while she let go of the steering wheel and latched onto my arm. We heaved together, up, over and back, falling onto the train's vibrating platform as the little car crashed into the pole and spun out, flipping end-over-end down the dirt road behind us.

"Mathew 7:14," she gasped. "Strait is the gate and narrow the way."

I panted and said something about the quick and the dead, and we made our way through the rear door of the observation platform into the interior of the coach.

❧

We quickly found our gang, but no sign of Nikkita.

"Haven't seen her," Walt said with mild concern.

"That's nonsense," I answered, running my fingers through the white streak in my hair, hoping to become more presentable. "Where could she be?"

"Probably waiting for Kaminski, for some reason," Ian said.

"I donna like it," Molly stated, her own hair a glorious crimson tangle.

Poole rested next to her, eyes closed.

"There are too many of us now who know about Goldenharz," Walt said in hushed tones. "Perhaps they've given up the chase."

I pointed to the tattered sleeve of my jacket. "Does this look like they've given up? They need those documents back. It's our only solid proof of the missile base."

"We'll be in Paris soon," Ian said. "Poole doesn't appear to be improving with time, so I've wired ahead for medical attention."

It still didn't add up.

'*Someone is lying*,' the Noir Man said.

I wondered sarcastically what else was new.

"I've got one for you," Norm said.

"Not now, please," I answered.

"No," he said, getting to his feet and edging past Walt and Ian. "Come with me a minute, will you? I'll tell you at the back of the car." I really didn't feel up to it, but he waited for me to calm down and follow him away from the rest of our group. He kept his voice low and didn't sing. Instead, he whispered, "I saw a woman like you described get off the train at the Nancy station. She was with a dumpy, old guy, and she didn't look happy."

"Was the guy soviet military or something?"

"Don't think so. As the train left, they met another man who could have been our old friend, Fake Fleming. It was hard to get a good look at his face."

This new information refused to fit into my head. They were here and then they weren't. Now you see 'm, now you don't. I was beginning to feel more and more like a spectator at a circus or magic show. Suzi would have figured it all out in a flash, but she was six or seven time-zones away.

When Norm and I came back to join our friends, they were attempting to compare details, updating our strategy and tactics.

"Did ya call fur backup?" Molly asked Ian.

"Did you?" Ian asked Walt.

"I thought you had," Walt said.

"Me?" Molly asked.

"No," Walt said. "Him."

"Me?" Ian said.

It was like watching a tennis match. "I'm sorry," I said. "This whole espionage business is a big pain in my ass—if you'll excuse my French."

The train had picked up speed and was hurtling along at more than fifty miles per hour past what looked like tobacco plantations. Its harsh melancholy whistle echoed back from the wall of a deep cut in a hillside.

"Spy verses spy?" Norm asked.

The phrase caught Ian's attention. "Why do you say that?"

Norm just chirped, "*Mad Magazine*."

"The kid's as smart as a whip," Walt said.

"Bowling ball," I corrected. "Smart as a bowling ball."

"Sharp," Molly corrected. "Sharp as a bowling ball."

Norm couldn't resist. "Did somebody, I say, did somebody knock?"

"Want to go around again?" I asked

Everybody except Norm shook their head and grunted in the negative.

※※※

Based on what he'd read in the guide book, Norman determined we were near the Route de Vin with villages full of cobbled streets, Renaissance fountains, and hanging flower baskets. "To our west," he read aloud, "the lyrical landscape of castle-topped crags and the mist-enshrouded Vosges Mountains glides into view."

I noticed we were speeding past green signal lights on poles next to the tracks. "You see those green lamps?" I asked him. "I'm pretty sure they mean the track is clear and it's okay to go ahead."

Norm seemed amazed by this. "So that's why he's called the Green Lantern."

The wound in his leg was healing nicely, probably due to Molly's dedicated care. Poole, on the other hand, was fading fast, almost delirious. I'd figured she should have recovered much more by now, but somehow we were losing her. Perhaps her age? She drifted in and out of a deep slumber, mumbling, at times. There were pin pricks on the inside of her left arm where they had administered something into her veins.

"I should have anticipated this," Fleming said, as concerned as the rest of us. "They've been drugging her in a way I haven't seen in years. To get her to talk, they've been pumping her full of something for days now."

"Sort of priming the pump?" Norm asked.

"But she seemed fine when we found her," I said. "Relatively speaking. Finer than this, anyway."

"Yes," Walt mused. "Her condition is getting worse."

"Antidote," Poole whispered through dry lips. She stared deeply into my eyes. "Need antidote."

A cold icicle dribbled down my spine.

"She's been infected with something," Ian said, rubbing the back of his neck.

"Then they must have been giving her the antidote while she was held at the opera annex," Walt added.

"Infected with what?" I asked, dumbly.

"Very shrewd," Ian concluded. "Without the antidote, she'll suffer and probably die."

"Some rescue," Norm said.

"Infected with what?" I asked again.

"Lord knows," Molly replied.

"We've got to get her to a hospital," Walt said.

"Do you think it's contagious?" Norm asked.

No one answered.

"Yeah, I know," he went on, looking from one woman to the other. "Lord knows."

The train gave a long whistle and began to slacken speed. It was a few minutes after five o'clock, and we were coming into the city of Reims. I knew that in 1945, Nazi Germany had surrendered unconditionally here to Eisenhower. With a jolt and a screech of the couplings, the express slowed to a walking speed and finally, with a sigh of hydraulic brakes and a noisy whoosh, ground to a stop.

I heard bells ringing out from the nearby Reims cathedral and remembered again that it was Sunday. I thought of Suzi and how we'd spent our previous Sabbath attending her church service. Why had she declined to come with me on this trip? Considering all that had happened in the last few days, I took heart in the fact that she hadn't come after all. But I missed her and couldn't wait to get back home again, away from counter-counter-espionage foolishness.

A double whistle sounded. There was a lurch and a diminishing crescendo of electric hums from the engine up front and the train began to move. Our car jerked harshly into line and we were pulled forward. I saw Fleming rushing back aboard from making more phone calls. Molly joined me as I slid open the window to crane out into the increasing wind and we began to glide past the station platform.

Within the small crowd of people looking back at us, I thought I saw Yuri's head turn a few compass points in our direction.

"Damn." Had they caught up again? I tried to point him out to Molly, but we were screeching around a bend now, and I couldn't be sure of what I'd seen.

How had I ever been fooled into accepting him as Ian? His complexion was darker, his hair was whiter, and those calculating eyes…

The real Ian Fleming came easily down the aisle, despite the increasing movement of the train, his hands never touching the edge of the seats. "I've called ahead for medical attention when we reach Paris," he informed us.

"They should be meeting us there in about an hour and a half."

The train was hitting her stride on a flat, open stretch of track. With a slight rocking from side to side, she was touching sixty miles an hour, roaming across trestles, flying through small villages, and hurtling past signals indicating open track ahead.

Norm came over to where I sat and tried to get me to recite a lyric from *Rhythm on the River*, but I wasn't in the mood. "Jeez, Norman," I said, perhaps too harshly, "that song is as old as Arthur Godfrey."

The train shot forward like an immense cannonball, and Ian and Walt were arguing again.

Fleming said, "I always thought you looked like that tall chap who appears with Lou Costello."

"Costello is a gangster," Walt answered, fidgeting with an unlit cigarette and book of matches.

I called over to them, "You guys are starting to sound like Allen and Rossi."

"Who?" Walt asked.

"I think he means Martini and Rossi," Ian said. "A brand of Italian vermouth."

Walt shook his head, came to sit beside me, and stared out the window. "Train rides are usually good for the soul," he said. "It was on a train ride that I first dreamed up Mickey."

I thought about asking him his middle name, but instead said, "What's your favorite movie?"

He considered it more seriously than I'd intended. "Anything by—" He puffed out air. "—Doug Fairbanks, Sr., I guess. Why?"

Romanesque churches and medieval market towns crept by, flashing a station sign that read, *Marne-de-Vallie*.

"You're still keeping something important from me, aren't you?" I said. "Detectives don't like that."

He puffed air again, as if clearing his conscious. "This area reminds me of what Anaheim used to look like." He avoided my statement by staring out the window at the passing show. "Be nice to someday build another Disneyland here close to Paris." His eyes seemed duller, his shoulders more slumped. "Maybe get NATO to fund it, partly."

Another sign streaked past in front of the fields and foothills. *Paris – 32 Km.*

"I've always wanted to see more of the world." He sighed. "Get out and maybe chuck it all and not come back." His grin came slowly, even now when he was intentionally being obscure with me.

I clinched my jaw to keep from cursing and watched the hurrying landscape. Summits crowned with ruined castles coasted in the distance. I had to admit that it was the most beautiful countryside I'd ever seen, but I couldn't wait to get to the end of the line in Paris, where physicians waited to attend to Agent Penny Poole's weakening condition.

I would have sold my soul right then for the taste of a taco and a cold Pepsi. Hell, I'd even've settled for a green bottle of 7-Up.

ᴄⱲᴏᴄⱲᴏ

Our golden journey finally ended in the rain a little after seven o'clock in the darkening evening. The efficient TEE transportation came to a stop at the Gare de l'Est, between lines of both rusting and gleaming locomotives. We walked down the platform and into the overarching and echoing iron and stone station half the size of the Olympic stadium back home. The scene, which should have been filled with the joy of victory, was bland and depressing from the late hour and the dank weather outside.

When the ambulance arrived with its up-and-down wailing siren, Walt and Molly guided Poole and Norm to its open back doors.

I was relieved. And tired. And sore. And pretty much done with the whole affair.

Then I saw the nun.

CHAPTER 24

Only she was not a nun. I'd know those harsh, smoldering eyes anywhere. She reached around Ian's neck and pulled him backward, tipping him off balance, and now had a hand with a cloth over his face.

It wasn't until Yuri Kaminski stepped over to twist Fleming's arm behind his back that I knew fully that our two pursuers hadn't given up the chase. They seemed unstoppable with unlimited determination and resources, for they kept showing up along our route regardless of what we did or where we were.

The handgun concealed beneath Nikkita's nun's habit accentuated their determination. This felt like their last chance to get the Goldenharz plans away from us, and, as I watched, Yuri pulled the documents from Ian's breast pocket. There was only one thing to do. I dashed forward and called out in a deep, authoritative voice: "Help. Police. Stop that man and that—nun!"

Several evening travelers halted and stared around. A few people ducked. One or two started running away.

Molly pushed me aside and charged forward, gun at the ready, giving out with, "My hands to fight and my fingers to do battle." A Biblical battle cry.

Nikkita thrust Ian's body into Molly's path, causing the trim British agent to swerve to avoid striking Fleming. It was just enough to allow the Soviet agent time to aim, fire and hit the young girl in the arm, causing her gun to skid along the pavement and drop over the side of the station platform.

I didn't have a weapon or a play, but I still moved in anyway. The two Russian operatives were already nearing the entrance of the gare, making their way into the street with the incriminating evidence.

A knife flew from behind me and high over my head. I ducked reflexively and looked back. Molly had tossed it, not to try and hit them, but to give me something to use in my pursuit. I snatched it up and continued on, seeing that Norm had come to her side. I gave them both an "Okay" with my thumb and forefinger, not caring if it was considered obscene gesture in this country.

Passing the prostrate Fleming, I smelled bittersweet chloroform and heard him shout, "For godsake, get those damned documents back!"

For a second, I flashed back to a time when I'd gone long during a USC football game, the lone receiver who had to make the play and win the game. Then I snapped back to the dark, wet rush of traffic outside the station where pelting rain struck my face and hunched back, causing me to jump back for fear that I'd been shot.

The only thing that dribbled down my head and chest was a cold Parisian drizzle on the Rue du Faubourg St. Denis. Could they make these street names any longer or more complex?

Outside the station and farther up the rue, I caught sight of a nun's black garment flapping in the breeze past a green flashing cross outside what looked like a drug store. I hustled after it, along a high stone wall to my left that concealed the train yard from view. I reversed the knife and tucked it up my sleeve to likewise conceal it from the small amount of public that I passed in the evening's downpour.

I moved up the street, past a butcher's shop next to a glass-blower's establishment. Two prostitutes and a mime stood huddled together smoking in the sheltered doorway. Apparently, Los Angeles wasn't the only land of fruits and nuts.

A shrill train whistle called from the other side of the stone wall. Wisps of steam rose from metal grates in the sidewalk, into the chilled October air. Another church bell rang out in the distance, signaling the end of Sunday services.

Someone came galloping up fast from my rear. I turned, ready to defend myself or explain to the French police, but saw that it was Norman, walking quickly and pretty well, considering his weak leg.

He raised the cane in my face and shouted through the rain, "They got Molly. Get them!" and limped past me, as if I were a parking meter cemented in the pavement.

I charged ahead and caught up with him at the intersection with Rue du Terrage whatever that was. "Is she dead?"

"Just wounded," he said, not waiting for the traffic light to change.

"Hey, stand down," I yelled. "Let me handle it." But he dashed between two oncoming cars and a splashing bus speeding from the other direction.

I put my head down and followed like an obedient pup.

We hurried in front of a Romanesque church with a huge clock mounted between two dripping towers. When we reached the other side of the street, I pulled him to me. "Stop. Go back."

"Nothing doing." There was fire in his eyes. He was like a new man—one I wasn't sure I knew. "I'm sick of sitting by while everybody else gets involved. Don't try and stop me, Mr. Wade."

Before I could answer, I saw yet another person coming up from behind us. The flashing traffic and pouring rain obscured my view, but I hoped it was the local johndamns.

Norm pulled away from me and pointed in the opposite direction, up a shadowy street. "Look. They're going down those steps."

He was right. It didn't matter who was behind us—the local cops or another player in the game. We couldn't afford to lose the Russian agents.

Forging ahead through the shower, we came to an entrance of the Paris subway, blocked off by metal railings. An ornate sign identified it as the Chateau Landon metro station. A more modern sign seemed to explain why it was closed down. *Ferme de Construction.*

"Are you sure they went down there?" I asked, not happy about going underground again.

Norm didn't answer. He was busy swinging his injured leg over the barrier and rotating his body to start down the stairs.

Water dribbled off my nose and lips. I did what I'd been doing reluctantly for over a week—I followed.

We descended a dozen wet steps and turned left along a tiled corridor. Our squishy footsteps echoed off the plastered walls of the enclosed tunnel. I stepped over bundles of two-by-fours and long rods of rebar. Stacks of red bricks and wooden crates lined the way as we pressed through a bank of turnstiles. Cables and tubing ran along the floor, ready to be installed near an open cavity that was draped with a brown canvas cover.

I listened and peered beneath the canvas. Nothing. Just darkness and the sound of dripping water.

Norm hobbled past a compact piece of digging machinery and hissed at me. "I hear them farther on."

The lights were dim and far apart, held in wire cages strung along drooping extension cords.

Now I heard footsteps again, but I couldn't get a bearing on whether they were in front of us or behind.

I caught up to Norman as we entered the cavernous underground station with its long line of double tracks set low in a wide deep trench. The ceramic ceiling curved up and over our heads, stretching across the tracks which vanished into the darkness in both directions.

Norm looked winded. I had to give him high marks for courage, but he was risking too much. If he folded on me now, we could both wind up dead.

'*In the rain, far from home*,' the Noir Man added.

"I'm the one in charge now," someone said in a muffled voice that resounded off the walls in front of us.

I attempted to adjust my eyes in the partial darkness.

Nikkita and Yuri were at the other end of the half-repaired Metro platform, on our side of the tracks. They had the documents we wanted and were arguing. Probably due to the fact that they'd trapped themselves in this hole and would have to come back this way to escape.

All we needed to do was to wait them out, but Norm didn't look like he'd make it without a nice long rest, and soon.

"Stay here, pal," I ordered, settling him into a crevice between a stack of plastic pipe and spools of copper wire and rubber tubing. "Keep down and let me handle this."

I picked up one of the thin pipes as a weapon and hefted the knife in my other hand. The pipe felt too light-weight, not sturdy enough for good defense. The knife felt tiny, compared to their guns. I found a short shovel instead, and slid the knife into the back of my belt, starting to move out, hoping to get help, just as Yuri said, "They'll never believe you."

I froze, until I realized he was addressing Nikkita.

She held the papers in one hand and a gun in the other. The gun was mine and it was pointed at Kaminski's chest. "And they'll never forgive *you*," she said. "The target needs to be Paris *and* London."

"I've had all I can stand of your back-stabbing ambition," Yuri replied. "You are holding me back and you know it. It ends now."

There was a blaring shout from behind us all, way back at the tunnel's entrance. It was enough to distract the woman, who suddenly saw me standing there, shovel raised and at the ready.

I flinched down, just as Yuri brought up his own gun and fired directly into Nikkita's dark cloaked figure, below her left knee. She went up in a sudden ball of fire and debris that jolted my ears and eyes, kicking me back into a pile of ceramic tiles and plastic pails.

Explosives, I thought, in the compartment of her

false leg. She'd been blown to hell in bite-sized pieces, and I could have sworn I heard Max's voice calmly confirm it. "Exactly."

Again, I'd been driven against something so solid that it knocked me nearly senseless. The room started to spin like a grand carousel, picking up speed. I wanted to get off. Nauseous and half blind, I felt something oozing from the back of my battered head.

Then, through a cloud of dust, smoke, and tears, Yuri came stalking in my direction. His face was streaked with dirt and blood, hopefully his own. But his gun hand was steady and pointed between my eyes.

I tried to raise the arm that still held the knife, but it wouldn't budge from the floor. I couldn't look away from Yuri's wicked smile and the vein pulsing in the middle of his forehead. I'll bet he hadn't smiled like that since the invasion of Poland.

His tobacco-stained teeth were enormous, ragged, and ready to suck the blood from my neck. I giggled, knowing that I was slipping out of reality from too many hits to the head.

The ringing in my head was like a million locusts. Otherwise, it was another silent movie, as I watched Yuri mouth something that looked like, "You always wanted to have Paris..."

Part of me fought back. "You know, I hate these rainy days," I said, half gasping and unsure that he could even hear me. "Brings out all the worms."

His eyes flared and an alien keening must have begun to slip from his lips.

My vision blurred, but I saw a bright metal nail sink into the left side of the killer's neck. The soft flesh under Kaminski's jaw absorbed the thin spike and let it protrude there like a short metallic arrow.

At first, he was stunned, unsure of what had happened. Then his smile returned, wider now and more ghastly than before. It was just a slight wound—nothing fatal. No serious harm or pain, considering the circumstances.

But it was enough to draw both his and my attention over to the stacks of building materials where I'd left Norman.

My pal stood upright, holding a makeshift weapon he'd constructed. He had strapped a plastic pipe to the length of Karloff's cane. There were rubber tubes dangling from the tip of the walking stick, like those of a spent speargun, where the metal spike had been pointed and launched at Yuri's neck.

The modified zip gun had halted Kaminski's intention to shoot me, but it wasn't enough to completely stop him. The mad Russian still had the upper hand.

I tried again to lift the knife and searched for the shovel, but failed. I struggled to get up, to speak, to kick out, to cry.

Yuri barked a laugh, knowing he would kill us both in the next seconds.

Then Norm threw something shiny out and over to land in the dark pit of the subway tunnel. A ball of reddish metal bounced and rolled along the track, uncoiling a thin length of wire that lead back to the spike in Yuri's neck.

The copper ball hit the subway's electrified rail, and Yuri instantly shuddered, silently screamed, and began to steam as he clutched the spike, yanking it from his neck. But his muscles seized and he couldn't let it go. He danced and smoldered to the steady, deadly flow of direct current. His legs buckled as he went rigid, and the gun in his hand fired impotently into the concrete walkway.

I felt, rather than heard, the bullets thud. The Yuri's body shook, sparked, and must have sizzled like a sixty-cent steak. The air was heavy with the tang of gunpowder, urine, and electricity. And then the copper wire melted through and the fallen body lay at rest.

I glanced back over to Norman and saw another person standing with him. The accumulated impacts to my head finally took their toll. I was slipping into insanity. My past and present blended into one swirling image and I knew I was leaving reality behind. The man next to Norman was my old boss, Mr. P.

CHAPTER 25

I was still weak, but could get out a complete sentence. "What are you doing here?" I asked.

Mr. P mouthed, "Groucho sent me." There was a fifty-percent chance that he wasn't kidding.

My brain drifted for a second and I latched onto the fact that he was all wet. Literally.

Norman came over and leaned into the Old Man.

"Nice zip-gun," I told Norm. "Plenty of zap in that arrow, too."

He smiled at my compliment, and I thought I heard him say. "I'm going to call it The Tingler." It didn't seem to bother him that he'd just killed a man, but he'd saved me. "I did it for Uncle Leo," his faint voice declared. "Does that make us full partners now?"

"Yeah," I said, still groggy. "Wade and Archer. Defenders of Justice."

Mr. P started to help me up, and I began to fully understand what he was saying. "Seriously, Stan, Walt called me. When he told me about Poole, I knew I had to be involved."

"Oh?" The back of my head was still wet and sticky.

"I flew over a few days ago, but missed all of you in London. I've been following ever since."

"Welcome to the club," I said, trying and failing to dust off my arms and legs.

"You guys get around," the Old Man remarked.

"So it was you that Norm saw at the Nancy train station with Nikkita?"

"Yes, I got the upper hand and ushered her off the train before she could harm your party, but her number-two man caught us there. They managed to get away from me before I could alert the local authorities."

I wondered aloud how he'd managed to stay on the trail.

"Ask Walt," he said. "I caught a car and followed them, racing here to find you running down the street in the rain."

So the bad guys had almost caught us twice and we'd slipped away each time by the skin of our bicuspids. We'd been living on the edge the whole time, traveling through French countryside.

"You came all this way? From Hawaii? Out of retirement? Why?"

"I couldn't sit this one out, if I could lend a hand and maybe save the day." He'd put on weight, age, and wrinkles around his eyes and mouth. "Looks like it didn't turn out that way, but I owed it to you and Poole, to at least try."

I digested this, suspicious again that I wasn't getting the full story. Perhaps I never would. "Who is she?"

But before he could answer, the Paris police arrived and took us firmly into custody, separating and questioning us for over twenty-four hours. That's the price you paid for almost blowing up their damn subway.

ℰↄℰↄ

I seemed to drift in and out of awareness in a Parisian hospital where accordion music played outside my window. What was *with* these people? I had to admit that the food was good, though.

There was a bandage on the back of my noggin and a blazing headache in the front that no amount of aspirin would dampen, so the doctors hooked me up to a sedative drip and told me to keep quiet. Poole was in another room down the hall, receiving treatment for her poisoning. Molly O'Dee was also in a room nearby, recovering from her shoulder wound.

Walt had contacted Interpol, who'd arranged for our

release from the local police, due to the important nature of the Project Goldenharz information. The incriminating papers had been destroyed in the explosion, but Ian had examined them thoroughly enough during the train ride that he could advise his government, and they could begin diplomatic action.

"The Reds will pull back the nukes," Fleming candidly advised our little group. "If not, your country's U-2 flights will provide everything needed to close down the operation, as well as the site."

"I have a special relationship with the world press," Walt conceded. "The Russians are bound to pull back and nothing will be said publically for perhaps fifty years. By then, it'll all be just a footnote in history. Otherwise, word of the threat will spread like wildfire and, well, let's just say that it's a small world, after all."

The next day, I had my head examined, yet again. But it didn't stop me from trying to get a full explanation from Walt about Mr. P.

"When we anticipated sending you to rescue Penny Poole," he said, "we decided to lay in some backup in case it didn't work out. That's part of the reason I called in your mentor from Hawaii."

"You could have told me," I groused, struggling to sit up straight in the slanting bed. For a second, I saw two Walts. I'd been hooked up to one of these dripping drug bags before, years ago after a case involving Dick Powell, and I hadn't felt as dopey then as I did now.

'*You're getting old*,' the Noir Man said.

I fought to keep my eyes from crossing.

Walt lit another cigarette and plucked a piece of tobacco from his lower lip. "As frustrating as it was for you, it was more frustrating for the Soviets. Nikkita Reed was killed by her own second-in-command."

"Who would have expected it?" I said. "They seemed as close as wallpaper."

Walt thought about it for a second. "She forgot that there's a Russian instinct to overthrow authority. In the end, I think Yuri pretty much cracked up from frustrated ambition."

Ian appeared from nowhere and agreed. "He saw his opportunity for advancement and took it. Ruthlessly. He wanted to become a sort of Soviet god."

Walt snickered. "If he's a god, I'm Mickey Mouse."

That one almost made my ears pop.

"When you're done with that brain," I said, "sell it to me, will you?"

Sometimes I get carried away. Probably comes from watching too many old movies, but I was beginning to succumb to the dull, oppressive effects of accumulated exhaustion, both physical and mental. My adventure in cloak-and-dagger world was nearing an end. And they could have it. No more Stan Wade, private spy.

Feeling beat in more ways than one, I was still compelled to ask, "How are the women? Are they going to be okay?" Blame it again on my misspent youth, watching movie heroes care more about others than themselves.

"Poole is making a full and rapid recovery," Walt answered. "And I told Molly that I had both good and bad news."

"Yeah?"

"The bad news was that she'd been shot in the shoulder, but she already knew that."

"And the good news?"

He took a long drag on his smoke. "The good news is that it's not contagious." Then he offered, "I've got something else important that you need to know, but it has to come from her, not me."

Her, I thought, drifting off to sleep. Her has got to be Suzi, my girl of the golden west.

 ⌀⌀⌀

Turns out, I was wrong. Her was Agent Poole.

She was recovering nicely. I was off the drip bag now, so I wandered down to her room. We had a brief chat beside her bed where high windows let late autumn sunlight stream across the polished floor.

The bandage at the back of my neck itched. I tried not to scratch while she explained about her stuntman cover during the making of *Ben Hur*. It was something I could relate to, since I'd once trained as a stuntman my-self. Before I left her room, I patted her hand. "You've done a great service for your country."

She sighed. "We cannot have peace without sacrifice. Take care of Walter."

Maybe she'd seen too many movies, too.

After I left her room, I made it a point to find Walter, who was sitting with Mr. P in the hospital's waiting room. The sun here shone brightly through green curtains and bounced off the chrome arms of the room's modern, awkward furniture. I would have liked to spend more time with the Old Man, but he was telling Walt that he had to get home to his wife, Carmen, who was ill.

"In a way," he said, "I should never have come, but…"

"Well, I wouldn't say that," Walt answered and then turned to me, asking, "How'd it go?"

"Fine."

"She's a brave woman," Mr. P said.

"You don't know the half of it."

"How long have you known her?" he asked Walt.

"Not as long as you have," Walt responded, adjusting his back in the hard, stiff chair.

The Old Man looked at me. "Do you find that you think about her much?"

"What? I just met her, a couple of days ago."

"Well, she had some reconstructive surgery after the crash, but…" Walt drawled.

"What are you saying?"

He paused and then went on. "She had amnesia for several years."

"She's kept undercover ever since." Mr. P added. "She's your mother, Stan.

I thought I must have misheard.

Even the Noir Man was speechless.

I rushed back to her room.

∞∞∞

I tried to absorb it all, sitting there for a long moment beside her. The sunlight came through the high windows at a different angle now. I was as uncomfortable as those chrome waiting-room chairs.

She'd stayed away for years, because she was afraid that I'd be, of all things, drawn into danger.

"Abandonment doesn't make a person feel safe," I told her.

She waited before speaking, and I could tell that it was hard for her. "We've lost so much time," she said, "that it's almost as if we're strangers."

"We are," I said. It sounded much colder than I'd meant it.

I had seen the results of the car crash back in 1949 and knew they were real. The Reds wanted to get a hold of my parents and their knowledge of aerial reconnaissance techniques that they'd been developing at the Lockheed Skunkworks.

Dad had died in the wreck, but—what I hadn't known at the time—was that Mom survived. The Feds replaced her body with a corpse as a ploy to fool the commies and protect my mother from further assaults.

She'd been a long time recovering, and the crash had affected her memory. In some respects, she was a clean slate—a different or new person that she and the government found useful in getting back at the Reds for a variety of reasons. Her desire for revenge and her love of country fed into involvement in small undercover operations and, after a few years, she became part of larger and longer missions for agencies like the CIA.

She'd operated like this for over a decade, with some assignments requiring deep cover and lasting more than a year. During one mission, Walt had employed her as an extra while the filming *Rob Roy* in the UK. There, stunt-double had functioned as her "minder" or handler. Stuntmen can go everywhere and are almost invisible, while remaining quickly available for changing conditions.

Yes, she had met Mr. P back in the 1940s. When I leaned forward and told her that the Old Man was planning to fly back to Hawaii soon, she seemed bothered by the fact, but wouldn't say why. I made a mental note to call and ask him about that, when we got back. Otherwise, I sat as still as a stone and listened to her go on.

"The agency kept me deep under cover," she apologized through damp eyes. "We needed our enemies to think that they had succeeded in eliminating both me and your father. So we used my engraved wedding ring to confirm that I was dead and to convince people that the female corpse in the wreck was mine."

"Convince people, including me," I said.

"That's the part I regret the most, Stanley," she said. "I know that it's been hard, but you've been in good hands all the time. They assured me of that and I like the way you've turned out."

She leaned her shoulder into my arm, and it was almost enough.

"I still have the ring," I said. "The police gave it to me with your other effects. It's in a safety deposit box in Hollywood."

"I've been watching you over the last few days, Stanley. Everyone thinks you're a smart-alecky jokester, but you're not. Those who really know you, know that you think things through."

I had no immediate response, except to say, "Uh, I guess."

Maybe, she *did* know me.

"When you were little, you used to listen to the *Lone Ranger* on the radio and run all around the house, shouting, 'Hi-yo Silver, away.' That's partly why your father and I sent you to that dude ranch for the summers. He was a good man. Not particularly patriotic. He had a higher calling."

I glanced around, attempting to get a handle on the subject. "I'm an adult now," I said, still feeling a little dizzy.

"I know." She sighed. "You and I are two different people now. We're connected, but distant. Strangers from a different lifetime."

I thought of Thomas Wolfe and decided he was right—you couldn't go home again.

"Our generation won't be around in twenty years," she said, wistfully. "We may not even make it to the American Bicentennial in 1976. Generations to come will want peace, perhaps at any price."

I realized that, in her own way, she was as dedicated to her cause as Nikkita Reed had been. But she was still my mom.

 ℰↄℰↄ

And, two days later, she left me—again.

When I went back to her room, I found it empty. It was almost too much to accept. Had she died, or...

A nurse told me in broken English that Mrs. Poole had been checked out. I rushed to find Walt, who explained that she had wanted desperately to go back to rescue her friend, Pyotr Popov, at the U-2 listening post behind enemy lines. It was urgent, since our intelligence service claimed that the double-agent there was about to be arrested by the Reds. "It's a debt she needed to pay and she didn't want anyone of us involved further," Walt said. "But this time, she'll have a full support team and should return in a few months." Or so he claimed.

I wanted to go after her. I never got a chance to tell her about my upcoming wedding. But Ian, ever the voice of upper-class reason and tested experience, convinced me that it would be better for all, if I waited and didn't interfere with the mission. "Lives are at stake," he counseled. "Let the professionals handle it."

Some profession. It reminded me of the way I typed my invoices—hunt and peck.

"You've been very lucky, so far," Walt added, "but as you've stated repeatedly, you're not cut out for this kind of work."

"Let our governments manage the situation," Ian said. "There can be no loose cannons or Wild West cowboys, now. This requires diplomacy."

Molly, arm still in a sling, said, "You canna risk putin herr in jeopardy by barragin in with both feet,"

They had all ganged up on me. Especially the Noir Man who said, '*Besides, it's all a lot of horseshit. Go stand down.*'

And in the end, I decided not to decide. Instead, I'd participate in the sorrows with grace, like an adult.

Ian and Molly soon left for England on more secret government business. They were needed there for an assignment involving the general election that would take place in a few days, on Thursday, Oct eighth. "So sorry. You understand. There's a good chap."

Molly blew me a kiss.

Before he left, Fleming gave me two more pieces of

advice. "One, when you finally reach my age, Wade, try your hand at writing. You won't regret it. And two, like the man said, eat your vegetables."

Jeez.

CHAPTER 26

Norm, Walt, and I sat through endless meetings, rehashing everything that had happened in Berlin and our trip to Paris. Eventually, we were advised to keep our mouths shut and allowed enough freedom to visit a few of the city's sights, while officials checked our facts. We were accompanied on our day-trips by an agent named Gerard Klein, a Frenchman who was also another science fiction writer. They seemed to be everywhere, like pod people.

The main tourist season had just ended, so many of the city's attractions were closed for repairs, or on limited hours. We saw some stunning stained glass right next door to the Paris police headquarters and way too many paintings and statues in the Louvre. We stumbled into some guy making a movie about a face without eyes or something, and that made me miss Hollywood all the more.

The following Monday, October twelfth, everything was cleared and we flew to NYC, where I drank my first Pepsi in weeks, proving Thomas Wolfe wrong, after all. Walt insisted on another train ride, so we arrived at Union Station in LA late the next day. Suzi met me there, all fresh-faced and smiling, in a thin white cotton dress that matched the color of her hair and a gorgeous tan that accentuated her blue eyes. I hugged her so hard, her back cracked, but she laughed with delight.

We rode to her apartment in her car and spent the night together. Very together.

"I kept busy, while you were gone," she confessed, fluffing up her pillow. "Want to know what I worked on?"

"Sure."

She set a thumbnail between her teeth. "I investigated a plagiarism suit for a man named Cussler, the creative director at a Denver advertising agency."

"Sounds dull," I said. "But it pays the bills, right? Let me look at you again."

"I got your flowers," she said. "Where were you?"

"Where I wished I weren't. I missed you, hugely. Let me hold you again."

She gave me a kiss that knotted my socks.

Nuzzling her behind an ear, I said, "Let me smell you—again."

Somewhere the McGuire Sisters were singing "Sincerely."

"Let me taste you," I demanded softly.

"Hold on a minute, big boy," she said, wriggling free. "We need to talk."

I ran my tongue around my teeth. "About what?"

She got up and said that she was feeling much better now.

I looked at her carefully. She seemed to have lost weight, but otherwise I hadn't a clue.

"I'm sorry that I didn't go on the trip with you," she said, looking away. "I wasn't sure, so I didn't say anything to you."

I sat up. "About what?"

The words spilled out of her mouth. "I thought I was going to have a baby—but it turned out to be a false pregnancy."

My thoughts suddenly started shooting all over the place.

"It's okay, Standy. We'll get it right. You'll see."

There weren't any words to express my feeling then, or at least none that my dull brain could come up with. I was numb for several seconds and the floor seemed to slant as I got to my feet and came around to her.

"Are you okay?" she asked, clutching my arm and almost cutting off the blood flow. "You're worried and breathing funny."

"What, me?" I almost gasped. "I'm fine. Yeah, fine.

How about you? I mean— psychologically—"

"I'm fine, too. Now. Things don't always work out the way we hope," she said, easing back into my arms. "But hope is all we have, sometimes. Hope for the best. And, sometimes, not often, your hopes come true."

I swallowed and studied the fascinating patterns in the carpet.

"Hey, are you listening?" She nudged me with a bare shoulder. "I love you."

I stared at this achingly beautiful woman. "Me, too."

Somewhere Connie Francis sang, "Lipstick on your Collar."

"Were you a good boy over there? Did you behave yourself with all those French girls?"

So I told her about meeting my mom.

She listened like she always did. Calmly.

"I found her and then I lost her again," I concluded.

"I know, baby," she said and pulled me to her. We stayed that way for about a hundred breaths. "You'll find her again. Or she'll find you. When she's ready."

"Time wounds all heels," I said and felt myself getting madder and madder all over again. "You know, I'm pretty fed up with Walt. He lies, hides the truth, and gets people into trouble."

She agreed. "You could have been killed over there and never have come back."

"I know. That's part of the reason I'm so upset with him."

She sat on the bed next to me and pulled her feet up under her tanned body. "You realize, of course, that he could have died there, too."

Damned if she wasn't right. Walt *had* risked it all. And for what? To rescue a valued agent? To defend the American way? To help me make contact with my mom?

"I guess, I still need to talk with him," I said. "He had a lot more on the line, than I did."

She shifted the subject to something more upbeat. Our wedding.

"I've decided I'll be a June bride," she announced, smiling in a way that always made my knees weaken. "I've done some planning and checking and it's all coming together, except I don't yet know how we'll be able to pay for it all. That's your job."

"Mine?"

"You're a great detective. You figure out how to pay for it all," she challenged playfully.

I grinned back at her, and her expression shifted to one of mild concern.

"Did you read any of those Saint stories, where he robbed from the crooks?" I asked, reaching for my trousers.

"Uh...yeah?'

"Well, this is something like that," I said and dribbled four nice-sized diamonds into her palm.

That earned me the kind of kiss that unknotted my socks.

⌘⌘

Suzi drove us through Beverley Hills just for the sight of it all. I saw a guy standing on his Jag to wash the top of his Caddy. On the way to the Brown Derby, my fiancée hummed a tune that I didn't know. "It's the theme from a new Doris Day movie, *Pillow Talk*," she said. "All the rage this week, and I like it."

"Me, too."

A colorful evening sky reflected the California orange sunset, as we pulled into the parking lot behind the restaurant. I scanned around and discovered that my Thunderbird convertible was missing from where I'd left it. Damn! Probably stolen. I loved this crummy town.

Lex and Sonny arrived seconds later in a '56 Imperial with a flame job painted on the front bumpers and hood. It was good to see them join us for dinner, and I almost kissed the old battleaxe when I saw her, but Sonny's scowl stopped me.

Among the two women, there was passing talk of a double wedding.

"Congratulations," I told Sonny. "I'm not sure how we do it, but I'm all for it."

The wise oriental barkeep grunted. "Reception at the Blue Phrog."

"Just don't invite Tony Bennett. Suzi hates him."

"Wait fifty years," he said sagely.

Inside the Derby, the thirtieth anniversary celebration

was still in full swing. Crepe and balloons hung from the ceiling. Big band music played softly from hidden speakers. We saw Sandra Dee seated with Ed Wynn. A guy who looked like Audie Murphy stood with a girl who looked like Betty Page among some of the most valuable people in Hollywood—tourists.

Norman was there already, hanging around a buffet table. When he caught sight of us, he rushed over to say that Walt had offered him a job. "He thinks I have great potential," my pal gushed, popping a cherry tomato into his mouth. "Holy socks!"

I let that exclamation go by the wayside without comment, because it sounded almost like something even I'd say.

Norman then asked, "You ever notice that in the movies or on TV, nobody ever watches television, unless they're in a bar, or something."

As normal with Norm, I wasn't sure where this had come from or was going. But I caught sight of Edd Byrnes walking in from the sandwich shop and it gave me an idea for a great answer. "Don't you ever watch George Burns's show? He has a TV that lets him watch the other characters without them knowing."

"Nice," Suzi said. "Parents could use something like that to monitor their sleeping children."

"Yeah?" Norm said and started stirring a celery stick into a bowl of cream cheese. "I'll have to give that concept some heavy consideration."

I didn't have the heart to tell him about the cameras in Dick Tracy's cruisers.

Lex nudged my sore shoulder. "Sometimes, I think that kid's so dumb, he'd stand forever in front of a stop sign, waiting for it to change."

I squeezed the bridge of my nose with a thumb and finger.

I realized that I was back in the smog, and my sinuses were back in full operation. But there was no place like home and, after all that had happened in the last few weeks, the world seemed a brighter place. Nothing had, as yet, been blown sky-high. The news headlines declared that the British elections were safely over and Prime Minister Macmillan's Conservative Party had won a sweeping victory. So had our local ball team, the Dodgers, who were flying home in triumph from the World Series.

'*Yeah, but,*' the Noir Man said, '*the Soviets hit the moon again with another rocket. That's twice now. The game has changed, again.*'

But I was back home with friends now. And I'd had enough of this dark thinking.

I told the Noir Man, "Well, ah, well that's just swell, Harvey. Now go lay down, you old pooka. Stop being smart, and try being pleasant. I recommend it."

Over the restaurant's signature dessert of grapefruit cake, Suzi said that there had been a call for me while I was in the shower. Something about director John Ford, wanting me to investigate a murder on the set of *The Al-*

amo. As dinner ended, the gang planned to go over to Dorothy Lamour's house to enjoy popcorn and out-take footage from *The Road to Hollywood*.

While I was counting up the bill, the owner of the Brown Derby, Robert Cobb, stormed over to our table, quite upset that I'd been gone from my security job here for the last two weeks.

I wasn't much bothered by his rant, having expected and even planned for it accordingly. "Mr. Cobb," I told him, folding my napkin. "I was on a vitally important mission for our government. And if you don't believe me," I continued, gesturing to a man seated on my left, "just ask President Eisenhower, here."

Cobb had met a ton of famous celebrities in his time, but he now stared open-mouthed at the smiling man with the high forehead, who sat with our party, quietly waiting for this moment. The restaurant owner gushed like a ten-year-old, shaking hands and asking for an autograph on the back of a menu. He didn't know that Ike was really the impressionist, Frank Gorshin, in town to appear in an episode of *Mr. Lucky*, called "The Last Laugh."

Sometimes you tell people the damnedest things, hoping they'll believe you.

The Facts Behind the Fiction

Goldeneye: Ian Fleming's Jamaican retreat where all the Bond books were written.

Ska & Bob Marley: Precursor of the Twist and Reggae.

Hiller Flying Platform: Tested and used by both the US Army and the Office of Naval Research, you can view this device in action on the internet.

U-2 flights over USSR: May 1, 1960 the soviets shot down Francis Gary Powers and brought back the chill to the cold war.

Paris: City of Light, Disneyland for Adults and site of the proposed Peace Summit, cancelled after the U-2 incident.

Boris Karloff: Sweet guy.

Gitmo: A little piece of American culture in Cuba's south end. Nice, rocky beaches, very few crowds.

Mickey Cohen: Dapper, diminutive, and deadly LA gangster.

Ben Hur: The most expensive movie made to date – $14 million – released 11/18/1959.

Frank Gorshin: Intense actor who became a riddle to television viewers, old chum.

Errol Flynn: Hollywood heartthrob who would suffer a heart attack and die a few weeks after the events told here.

Elvis Presley: Another heartthrob who would later yearn to be a federal investigator.

Whirlybirds & Bob Gilbreth: Passed away in copter crash while fighting forest fire two years after the events of this story.

Lockheed Skunkworks: Secure aviation development area, north of Hollywood, where the U-2 and later the Stealth fighter were created.

The Bells are Ringing: Judy Holliday's and MGM's last great musical.

John Steinbeck: Author who travelled with Charlie.

Vogelsang: Site of Europe's nuclear-missile crisis. One of the Cold War's best-kept secrets, until files were declassified in 2012.

Taser: A later version of Norman's Tingler.

If you enjoyed

SPYFALL

Turn the page for a preview of

STARFALL

the next book in the Stan Wade Series

Coming from John Hegenberger and
Black Opal Books in 2016

PROLOGUE

I loved my job. I got threatened and shot at by the most interesting people. Today it would be another Hollywood star. Tomorrow? Maybe a mobster. Maybe a commie. Maybe even an astronaut. But today's assignment was to go and bring back a wayward starlet. Or so I'd assumed.

So I grabbed an early lunch and pointed my battered '53 Kaiser Manhattan toward Palm Springs, cruising east on highway 111, past Cathedral City and Palm Desert. Eventually, the road snaked up a hill of boulders and rattlers to a swell hideaway spot. The low ranch-style house was a combination of Spanish and modern. I parked next to a chartreuse Caddy and checked the license plates. A hot, dry wind blew off the mountains and lightly touched up my hair. I hung my sunglasses on the rearview mirror and got out to approach the front entrance, listening to my footsteps crunch gravel.

I knocked, listened, and tried the door. It was part wood and part glass and all locked. I took off my jacket, held it to the glass, and struck it smartly with my right elbow. Now I could hear pulsating music coming from a room in the back of the house. I walked toward it.

She was dancing, arms and legs spread wide. A leopard-skin one-piece bathing suit. The pool on the terrace behind her moving body shimmered in the afternoon sun.

I lifted the needle from the LP on the stereo, and she staggered when the sound stopped, turning to raise a fit.

"All right, Annette." I sighed, jabbing a thumb over my left shoulder. "Party's over. Let's go."

She screeched and let fly with a heavy cut-glass tumbler that bounced off the wall behind me. I smelled expensive whiskey.

She charged forward with raised claws, so I lifted the record from the stereo and skimmed it at her, like one of those new Frisbees. I gently took hold of her right wrist, spun her around, and enfolded her tight until she stopped twisting and stomping. I nudged the phone receiver off the hook with my right knee and dialed "0" with my left forefinger.

From the corner of my eye, I saw Guy Williams come into the room, tightening an electric-blue bath robe. I raised the phone receiver to his handsome face. He stepped back, smiled, and bowed graciously.

This tough-guy persona was working fine for me and I figured this was going to be one of my better assignments. "Hello, operator? Get me Disney Studios. Hollywood. Stan Wade calling."

CHAPTER 1

And now, all I wanted to do was collect my fee.
Tuesday, March 24, 1959, I waved through the gates of one of the biggest little movie and television production companies in town and parked in a visitor slot next to the four-story factory, complete with its own water tower. *They'll put ears on that thing one of these days.*

Here, across sun-washed Burbank acres, pirates and frontiersmen, cartoonists and cameramen, accountants and actors toiled daily under the benevolent guidance of "Uncle Walt."

I'd worked a couple of jobs in the past for him and was here to see again today about money. Inside the fun factory, I slurped cool water from a stainless-steel drinking fountain and pressed the elevator's "Up" button to ride to Disney's office. As the mirrored interior doors slid shut, my reflection nodded at me and almost cracked a smile. Brown eyes with an arching eyebrow, dark hair with a streak of white, average build with the average face of an average office worker. Only this average guy hated office work, preferring to be out in the field, or on the street, or just about anywhere, except heavy LA traffic.

Walt, on the other hand, was a man of sixty, possibly a little more, and had a lot of powdery gray hair, a thin moustache, and a handsome dissipated face that was beginning to go pouchy. His suit was tan and his tie was brown. The exact opposite of mine. A white handkerchief peeped out of his breast pocket and the fingers of his right hand drummed the change in his pants pocket.

I jerked a pack of Luckies toward him so a couple cigarettes extended in his direction. "Worried about me?" He was a chain smoker and this was his brand. "By the way, isn't Annette still under age?"

He accepted a smoke and lit up from a desk lighter shaped like the Nautilus submarine—the one from his movie, not the one that went under the North Pole last year. "She's twenty-one." He exhaled. "And some security analyst you are. Didn't you figure out during the long drive back that the girl I sent you after is really just her stand in?"

I wasn't sure I believed him. He'd kidded me before, so I gave him my poker face. "Professional investigator, if you don't mind."

He took a deep drag, saying, "That still means you're only a PI. Hell, Stan, you need to think bigger. Quicker, too."

"Walt, she sat in the back seat the whole time and wouldn't talk. I dropped her off at the front gate and she stomped in without a word. Besides, you should know by now that I always get results when you hire me."

He stared for a moment at a framed photo on the wall beside a potted ficus. It was an old tintype of a steam engine crossing a high wooden trestle. "Maybe," he allowed.

"Look, you sent me out there and I brought her back alive and kicking. Scratching, too."

He let that go and rested a hip on the side of his desk. "She does Christmas parades and other events for us, where the public can't get close enough to tell the difference. Still, we can't have her running loose, like that. Bad for the company's overall image. Thanks for bringing her back, Stan. And thanks too for helping Fess with that blackmail thing last month."

I shrugged. "Always a pleasure. Just pay my bill and I'll be glad to keep watch over any of your cowboy heroes, anytime you ask."

"Humph. I've got another kind of hero that I want you to work on." My number one client went back around behind his desk and settled easily into a high-backed chair. "I have a featurette in development about weather satellites and another one about Project Mercury."

"Oa-kay." I'd read a little in the *LA Times* about the orbiting satellites which could track and maybe someday influence the weather. Sounded pretty far out there, literally. I'd also read about the test pilots that our country was assembling for the august challenge called Project Mercury.

Every branch of the military was being evaluated as part of America's program to launch a man high into the upper atmosphere where he'd circle—scratch that, orbit—the earth. If he was lucky, like that Russian had been, he'd come down in one working piece. I had to admit, it was a hell of an idea. The slide-rule boys insisted that we needed to do it or the Soviets would take over the world from on high and maybe even stake claim to the moon. Yep, pretty far out.

Walt got back up and straightened a picture on the wall that, as far as I could see, didn't need straightening. He mashed out his cigarette in an owl-shaped ashtray on his desk.

"You're still worried," I said, waiting him out. "What's all this space stuff got to do with you, anyhow?"

From a desk drawer, he pulled out his own pack of Luckies and lit up again. "I'm not going to get into that right now, Stan. Suffice to say that I've got a heavy investment in it. I need you to go up to Edwards Air Force Base to meet with Colonel Fielding Scott." He nudged a sheet of paper toward me across the polished surface of his desk. "He'll be expecting you. This will get you access to the base."

I scanned the paper. There was no indication that it came from Walt. It began and ended with a string of numbers like a coded telegram or a Christmas club account at the savings and loan.

"I still don't get it," I said. "All this for a space movie? Why am I meeting this guy?"

"In the past, when I've hired you, you've been discreet. I value the fact that you didn't ask me dumb questions."

"For a hundred dollars a day, plus expenses, right?" I wondered if he noticed that I'd just asked a question.

"Yes, well, we'll talk about those expense reports later. He gave me a lean grin, and I wished that it had been broader. "What I need now is an objective and confidential investigation into the death of a Mercury Project test pilot. You'll act under my direction and report back the details, plus whatever insight your investigation generates."

"Wait, now. Slow down." I held up my right hand, the one I used to scratch my head when I was confused. "Is this for real or are we talking about one of your movies? Who's dead and how?"

"I'm not the one you should be questioning," he said. "But the pilot's name is, or was, Albert Taffe. He was an air force captain stationed at Edwards, where he drowned."

"Drowned? Edwards is on the edge of the Mojave Desert."

Walt stared at me like he needed an antacid.

"Oh," I quickly said, "that's *why* you want me to investiga—"

An angry *buzz* sounded from an intercom box on his desk and a sweet Southern drawl said, "The people from ABC have arrived for your meeting."

Walt pushed a button on the box. "Put them in conference room B, Tommie. And let them know that I'll be right there." He snuffed out his smoke in the owl as I hesitantly got up to leave. "You have my private phone number, Stan. See Tommie for your check. You'll get the rest of details from Colonel Scott. Bring them back to me, along with your insight."

At the moment, my insight needed a telescope.

About the Author

John Hegenberger writes adventure, mystery, science, and horror fiction. Born and raised in the heart of the heartland, Columbus, Ohio, he is the author of *Tripleye* series and the *Stan Wade LA PI* series from Black Opal Books. Father of three, a tennis enthusiast, collector of silent films and OTR, hiker, Francophile, B.A. Comparative Literature, ex-navy, ex-comic book dealer, ex-marketing exec at Exxon, AT&T, and IBM, he has been happily married for 45 years.

Over the years, he's published two non-fiction books about collecting pop-culture movie memorabilia and comic books and sold half a dozen stories to magazines and anthologies. Follow his adventures at johnhegenberger.com and have fun.

CPSIA information can be obtained
at www.ICGtesting.com
Printed in the USA
LVOW01s0325171016

509044LV00011B/91/P

9 781626 944213